PITTSBURGH NOIR

EDITED BY KATHLEEN GEORGE

Published by Akashic Books
©2011 Akashic Books

Series concept by Tim McLoughlin and Johnny Temple
Pittsburgh map by Aaron Petrovich

ISBN-13: 978-1-936070-93-0
Library of Congress Control Number: 2010939107
All rights reserved
First printing

Akashic Books
PO Box 1456
New York, NY 10009
info@akashicbooks.com
www.akashicbooks.com

ALSO IN THE AKASHIC NOIR SERIES:

FORTHCOMING:

Fox Chapel

28

Allegheny River

Morningside

Highland Park

28

Lawrenceville

East Liberty

Bloomfield

Schenley Farms

Homewood

Wilkinsburg

Squirrel Hill

30

22

376

Forest Hills

Monongahela River

TABLE OF CONTENTS

PART III: UNIVERSITIES, PARKS, RECREATION

PART IV: NEIGHBORS WHO CARE

INTRODUCTION
PRIVATE MORALITIES, PRIVATE LAW

In 1996, my husband and I were on sabbatical leaves in the south of France. *And* the Steelers were playing in the Superbowl. How could we miss that? I located a bar in Monaco called Le Texan. Unfortunately, the Steelers were playing the Dallas Cowboys that time around, so when we got to the bar, the place was filled with braying people in Stetsons. One drunk man stood up and said, "Did anyone ever hear of *anything* good coming out of Pittsburgh?" The place was too noisy for him to hear me answer.

It was a should-have-won/could-have-won loss.

Not everybody in Pittsburgh is sports crazy, but most are. Scratch a Pittsburgher and you will hear about Bill Maze-roski's home run that won the 1960 World Series, the catch known as "the immaculate reception" by Steeler Franco Harris, the amazing year of 1979 when the Pirates won the World Series and the Steelers won the Superbowl. The Pi-rates, the Steelers, and the Penguins play out our personal dramas. *Didn't look possible and then he did it.* Or: *That show of anger was the thing that turned it around.* Or: *All in their hands and they got too confident.* Sports provides all kinds of possible narratives. And the best one keeps being the story of the impossible, the story of the underdog fighting back and winning.

Pittsburgh has its own story: It was built around three riv-ers, became a thriving center for the manufacture of steel, and attracted many immigrants to work the mills. Clashes between owners and laborers are part of its history, perhaps most notably the Homestead Steel Strike in which workers fought back when their wages were cut. It didn't work. Management won. The Carnegies, the Fricks, the Mellons lived here and spun gold. Italians, Czechs, Poles, and others sought solace in neighborhoods that were like villages within the city. The neighborhoods still carry the marks of their founding in the churches, bars, and restaurants that survive. There is Italian Bloomfield and the eponymous Polish Hill.

When the steel business faltered and died, "the smoky city" reinvented itself as a white-collar urban site, fueled by its thriving universities. It had been a place so dark with pollution in the steel days that men carried clean shirts with them to work in order to change during the day. Now you can *see* the hills, the rivers, the rhythmic skyline—and as the cameras are fond of displaying at sports events, the city is now glittering and beautiful.

Anybody moving to Pittsburgh learns pretty quickly that it boasts affordable prime real estate, three beautiful rivers, parks and monuments, a flourishing university and cultural life, major medical centers, and tight neighborhoods. It's been named more than once the most livable city in America. Young people who have grown up here get antsy, though, and move away. New residents who come in for a job or a school, surprised by what they find, often decide to stay. Former residents feel tugs of longing and move back. (Contributor Stewart O'Nan has moved back; contributor Hilary Masters is one of the people who discovered the city and stayed.)

What is Pittsburgh to *noir* and *noir* to Pittsburgh? We certainly have our rough streets and grisly murders. But dark crime stories depend on something in addition to killing. The best examples of the genre revolve around private moralities and private law; they are the stories of people pushing against real or imagined oppression. In *Pittsburgh Noir*, as in most of the novels and films that gave the genre its name, the real story is the dark underbelly of existence, the fear and guilt and rebellion and denial in regular people: the woman buying groceries, the man grilling hot dogs. Their secret lives.

I'd like to thank Mary Alice Gorman of Pittsburgh's Mystery Lovers Bookstore for spurring me to jump into this project. And I'd like to thank the contributors who've joined me.

I've snagged a story from the legendary (and anonymous, Pynchon-style) K.C. Constantine, as well as from Shamus Award winner Tom Lipinski and the multiple award-winning poet Terrance Hayes, who shows he can do fiction too. I invited esteemed fiction writers Stewart O'Nan, Hilary Masters, and Reginald McKnight to turn to crime, and they did so with distinctive voices and dark humor. No Pittsburgh collection would be complete without Lila Shaara, Rebecca Drake, Nancy Martin, and Kathryn Miller Haines, all publishing mysteries regularly to critical acclaim. Three stories come from exciting new voices who push the boundaries of the genre: Paul Lee, Carlos Antonio Delgado, and Aubrey Hirsch.

We'll take you to Bloomfield, the Mexican War Streets, Forest Hills, Fox Chapel, Schenley Farms, Carrick, McKees Rocks, Highland Park (a little-known unofficial marina), Wilkinsburg, East Liberty, Morningside, Squirrel Hill, Lawrenceville, and Homewood.

Here's to the black and gold; to the Allegheny, Monongahela, and Ohio; to Jonas Salk and Thomas Starzl; to Primanti's sandwiches and churches that sell pierogies; to all and everything that makes up the 'burgh.

Kathleen George
Pittsburgh, PA
March 2011

PART I

PRIME REAL ESTATE

PART 1

ATOM SMASHER

BY LILA SHAARA

Forest Hills

Y ou grew up next to a *what?*" the sweaty girl said. Hot was supposed to be synonymous with sexy, he thought, all that imagery of damp flesh and body heat. She looked damp all right, but on her it just looked like she'd smell bad if you got too close. Her hair was big and her accent jarring; he'd been living in Atlanta for seven years, ever since college. He'd grown used to soft Southern consonants and slippery vowels. The sharp angles of Pittsburghese grated on him now, along with her sweat-darkened tank top and spiky, lacquer-hardened hair. The air inside the bar was so steamy he thought he might faint. He imagined he looked as though he'd just come out of a hot tub himself.

"An atom smasher," he said. "It was built even before the atom bomb. They were smashing atoms together before they even knew that they could blow up the world that way."

"Huh," she replied, and he could tell that she didn't believe him; people seldom did when he told them this bit about his past, but he expected more from a local.

He said, "You can see it from Ardmore Boulevard. It looks like an upside-down teardrop."

She looked interested. "You mean the big metal ice-cream cone?"

"Exactly."

"Wow," she said. "I've seen it my whole life, and didn't

know that that was what an atom smasher looks like. Growing up next to that, you're lucky to be alive."

Ronnie hadn't expected her to want to have sex with him, and he was sad to find that it was in a way a relief. He had just moved back home, and amid the shame of it all was the practical problem of having nowhere to bring women. But he'd only been back a month, and though he'd gone several times to a bar that had been good to him in the past, he hadn't had to solve this particular problem as yet. He was not quite drunk when he returned to the house that was now partly his again. It was quiet; his parents were asleep. Thank God, he thought, and got a beer from the refrigerator.

He went upstairs to what used to be his bedroom; his parents had turned it into an upstairs den, with a large TV, a couch, and a small refrigerator. His father called it his "man cave," and he hadn't wanted to return it to his son. Now Ronnie was sleeping in a semifinished room in the attic, which was hot despite the window air conditioner, but he couldn't bear the thought of living in the guest room, which had wallpaper covered in ducks. The best thing about the conversion was a deck built off the second-floor room that hung high above the backyard. Ronnie went out the sliding glass door, and eased himself into one of his mother's old patio chairs, the kind with fat, if slightly mildewed, cushions. After a minute he got up again and brought some matches from the kitchen, and then lit two giant citronella candles that sat on the wide wooden railing. The mosquitoes here weren't as big as the ones in Atlanta, no matter what the locals wanted to believe, but they were bad enough when they were hungry.

He could see the silhouette of the atom smasher in the low horizon, unmistakable even in the gentle red light given off from the city center, eight miles away. He'd never heard it called the more modern term: particle accelerator. Compared to the ones they built now, it was minuscule. But he'd always been told that it was the first one ever made, and so it had an excuse for being a nuclear pipsqueak. Even so, the metal ice-cream cone was six stories high; it sat on top of a large, ugly bunker of a building constructed out of concrete and corrugated steel. The whole structure covered over an acre of land, the cracked and weedy parking lot surrounding it covering at least two more. The orange paint flaked off in handfuls, and there were few windows; it looked like the setting for a bad postapocalyptic film. Yet Westinghouse had tucked it away in this residential enclave, presumably so that many of its employees could live nearby and walk to work. Fortunately, the topography of his home town meant that he couldn't see the ugly bunker from the deck, only the metal dome itself.

Forest Hills was aptly named; virtually every backyard was a slope in one direction or another. His parents' house poked out of the hillside like a shelf fungus on a locust tree. The ancient Westinghouse complex lay off to his left, only four lots away. The old-fashioned Westinghouse tinker toy W painted on its side was eye level. He'd actually thought about taking the sweaty girl from the bar there after all this time. He'd already forgotten her name, and he'd never been attracted to her, other than in the basest, most pragmatic way, an opportunity, even if it wasn't particularly appealing. Man, he thought, it's been a long time since I've done it there. Remembering that none of the girls had been over seventeen, he thought, it was statutory rape, and I was too stupid to even know it. Maybe some of the girls' luck did rub off on me, since I never got caught.

In high school he'd been well-liked and thought handsome by enough girls that it had become accepted as fact by everyone else. But he hadn't been a star in sports or in anything else, and so his professional success had made coming home to his tenth reunion a pleasure. He still looked good, had a pretty wife and a career that many of his former classmates envied. He'd loved saying, "I'm a sports writer," over and over between sips of warm beer. "For the *Atlanta Journal-Constitution*. Had to move to the Sun Belt, but I'm still a Steelers fan." It had gone over so well that his dreams had rung with the social success of it for weeks.

But four years later, the wife was gone, as was the job—the price of being in a junior position in a downsizing industry. He still had a friend or two, though fewer than he thought. Print journalism is dead anyway, they all said. Do online stuff, they said. As though it were that simple; as though that was the way to get rich. But his boss had said, "Sorry, Ronnie, but you're not that good. My advice? Find a different line of work."

He'd received a mailing about the fifteenth reunion. The irony of not having to travel this time did not make him smile. Now he stared at the atom smasher and thought, this time maybe I can get it to work for *me*.

His mother said, "What a blessing that the sun's out," for the fifth time, as she pulled a five-pound package of hamburger meat from the refrigerator. It had rained for the last three days. Now the sky was empty of everything but a hot, white sun, the blue around it hard, like thick glass. It made Ronnie's head hurt to look at it; he'd been at the bar again the night before, and he had a hangover. It hadn't even been worth it; the available women had been either unattractive or uninterested. Now he followed his mother's orders, and spent the morning setting up chairs in the backyard and helping her shape the loose, wet meat into patties. At noon, she released him, saying, "Just don't make a mess anywhere."

He pulled a can of soda from the refrigerator and went upstairs to the second-floor deck. He sat, popped the can, and looked at the atom smasher, hanging above the trees beyond the yard. It looked like a huge, fat metal teardrop that was going the wrong way. Like a giant cried while standing on his head, he thought. Maybe I can get a job as a poet. Then he almost smiled, thinking, there's one of the few jobs that probably pays less than a newspaperman. He took a drink; it was too sweet. Root beer. He hadn't noticed what he'd taken from the kitchen. His mother always had a large stockpile of soda in case they had company, and today they were expecting a lot of it. She bought the stuff by the case, store brands that came in all the basic flavors: cola, ginger ale, root beer, grape, and orange. He wondered how they got away with using words that designated actual fruits. Orange was a color too, of course. But, he thought, the words are always followed by the microscopic amendment, *flavored drink*. Root beer used to be the boiled and carbonated syrup of the sassafras root. He knew because his Uncle Lou had made some when he was a kid. It tasted alcoholic to him then. Knowing his Uncle Lou, it probably had been fermented. The stuff in the can was mostly corn syrup and some unknowable chemicals that tap-danced on your taste buds and some sort of dye the color of shit. He drained the rest of the can. He thought, maybe I could get a job as a taste tester for crappy cola.

From the deck he could peek through the slats in the railing and watch the festivities without being seen. The basement door two stories below opened out to a brick patio some twenty feet square; it was dotted with a disreputable but solid collection of lawn chairs culled from sixty years of family gatherings. A gas grill the size of a player piano sat on a far corner of the patio, and his father was replacing the propane tank underneath it, something his mother had wanted him to do the day before, and had loudly wanted Ronnie to help him. Ronnie was relieved that his father had ignored her on both counts. His mother didn't seem to know he was up on the deck, and his seated position allowed him to be invisible from below unless he chose to poke his head up above the wooden railing.

Behind him, he heard the brushing sound of the screen door into the upstairs den, and turned to see his cousin Gary standing on the threshold. He hadn't seen Gary in several years, and his looks hadn't improved. Gary was a few inches shorter than Ronnie, and was usually heavier. Ronnie had always thought that Gary had a head the shape of a potato, though of course much larger; he thought about this now, since the resemblance had grown more pronounced with the years. Gary came onto the deck, a soda can in his hand as well, and sat down on a chair identical to the one on which Ronnie sat, white-painted rattan with cushions in a loud floral print. "So, Ronnie," he said, "how's it hangin'?"

Ronnie gave the automatic answer, rehearsed and perfected and enjoyed many times in their shared youth: "High and long, Gary, high and long."

Gary tipped his can toward Ronnie, who raised his, and they met with a satisfying *tink*. Ronnie remembered that Gary had had to stop drinking a few years ago. Two years? Three? He couldn't recall, nor could he recall any of the details his mother had told him, although he was pretty sure that Gary had ended up in rehab. Gary no longer had a wife, and the divorce was complicated by the fact that he had two kids, or maybe it was three; Ronnie couldn't recall the details of that either. Ronnie hadn't seen any young kids running around the backyard below, so he supposed Gary's ex had custody. Here at last, he thought, was someone who would also understand the meaning of bad luck.

Ronnie pointed to the atom smasher. "Any new plans to tear it down?"

Gary said, "No, and no one wants to buy it. They tried to get the Smithsonian to take it, but the damn thing's too big. Too expensive to trash it too."

"Is it still radioactive?"

"Supposed to be. If that wasn't all just scare talk to keep teenagers away."

Ronnie smiled. "Does it work? It didn't used to."

Gary laughed, and Ronnie could see that he was missing a couple of teeth. His mother had died of some kind of cancer when they were kids; now with his wife gone, there seemed to be no one monitoring his oral hygiene.

Gary sipped his can. *Cola* was written in blue letters on a red background. He said, "Sorry to hear about your troubles. But your mom's glad you're back."

"Thanks."

Gary nodded at the great inverted teardrop on the horizon. The summer light caught it so that it gleamed like the dull side of a sheet of aluminum foil. "You been back there?"

"What?"

"You know. You take any girls there?" He wasn't looking at Ronnie, but at the big teardrop.

"It's been a long time, Gary. I don't know any girls that are available. And worth it, if you know what I mean."

"You got your eye out, though, right?" Gary turned to face him, and he was still smiling. His face was sweaty. Ronnie wondered if he'd spiked the cola with something; Gary almost looked a little drunk.

"Sure," answered Ronnie.

"Sucks about your job. Sales sucks now too. Fuckin' economy." He said *ecawnomy*, and Ronnie tried not to find it annoying while Gary repeated, "Fuckin' economy." Then he got up abruptly, crunching the empty soda can with fat fingers, causing the rattan chair to twitch and rustle in unpleasant ways. "I'll be back," he said in a weak Austrian accent, and then disappeared through the sliding doors.

Ronnie heard voices from the front of the house, where his mother was greeting whatever neighbor or relative had just arrived. The number of people on the patio below was gently increasing, as was the volume of the voices. No one was looking up; most eyes were turned toward the grill where his father presided over a dozen or so fat sausages. Ronnie caught the smell, and it made him hungry.

His mother appeared from beneath the deck, leading an old woman by the arm. He recognized her: Mrs. Asch from three doors down. Skinny and saggy and gray, oh my, he thought. But then he watched his mother reach a welcoming hand out to someone behind old Mrs. Asch, another woman, but not an old one, and from what he could see of her, she was far from saggy or gray. She was tall and slender with a beautiful ass in tight white shorts, nice tan legs, bare between cuff and sandal, and a yellow tank top that fit snugly across round breasts. Her hair was brown and very curly and full, caught up in an attractively messy ponytail. He thought, she's got to have the face of a moose, with a body like that.

Gary came through the door again with a clatter as he accidentally nudged the vertical blinds that were pressed together in a skinny wad at the side of the door. He was carrying a compact blue cooler, which he plopped down beside Ronnie as though it was heavy. Gary opened it and the inside glowed gold, like pirate treasure. Gary pulled out two sweating cans of Michelob and handed one to Ronnie. The cool feel of it in his hand was delightful in the day's heat. Gary sat down again in the whispering chair, and together they popped the tops of the cans, tilted them at each other, and each took a sip. Both cans were empty within a few minutes. Ten minutes later, Ronnie was on his third, and Gary his fourth. Ronnie wondered how many the cooler could hold; every time Gary opened it, it glowed from within.

Ronnie was about to ask Gary to lean forward and identify the woman with the beautiful body when his cousin said, "You remember Josette?"

It took a few moments for Ronnie's neurons to reorient, and then the information clicked together—a face, a body, a smell, a voice. He said, "Josette Foyle."

"Yeah. Oh man. She came home for her mom's funeral last year, and she looked exactly the same, man. Exactly the same. Tits like basketballs." He waited for Ronnie to answer, but when he didn't get a response, he went on: "I 'member when you took her up there." He nodded at the great W that hung above them. "She was so fuckin' sexy. No pun intended." He grinned his gappy grin.

Ronnie grinned back, only slightly uncomfortable. The beer helped. "Yeah," he said. "She was something."

"How many times did you take her up there?" He said it *up air*.

"Only twice." That's all it took, he thought.

"Right, cause then her dad got that job where they moved away, somewhere overseas."

"Paris."

"Goddamn *France*," said Gary. "Couldn't pay me."

"If someone paid you, you'd go to fuckin' Shitsville," Ronnie said without giving it much thought. Old rhythms, like call and response. He thought, she was so happy it was all she could talk about. Paris, Paris, Paris.

"I already live in Shitsburgh," Gary said. Another old joke. Gary lived in Forest Hills, two blocks from his parents; the borough had its own mayor and so it technically wasn't the city. But everyone said they lived in Pittsburgh when it was easier, or when they were talking about sports. "Didn't she marry someone there and sort of become a Frog herself?"

"Yes," Ronnie said. "I thought you spoke to her when you saw her last summer."

"No." Gary shook his head. "She'd never remember me, bro."

Ronnie was starting to feel drunk. "She married a Michelin."

"A tire?"

"No. A person who's part of a family who owns a tire *company*."

"Shit yeah. That's right."

Ronnie drank more, sitting up straighter so that he could see over the railing. The girl in the tank top and shorts was talking to his Uncle Lou. She laughed at something Lou said. Ronnie still couldn't see her face, could only tell by the tilt of her head and a faint sound that seemed to come from her, that seemed to be laughter. And Lou was all smiles himself. Ronnie thought, she must be pretty.

Gary said, "Who else was there? Mary Galetti?"

"Oh. Yes."

"And Brenda Bergamo. Nia Petrandis."

Ronnie said, "Stacey Trelski."

"Yeah. Blond. Cute. Small."

"Yes," Ronnie said. "She's an actress now."

"Really? I never heard."

"She changed her name, and she's mostly been in horror movies. But she's done pretty well. She changed her name to Stephanie Thomas."

"That's her? Jesus, I didn't know." *I dinno.*

Ronnie added, "Nia got into Penn on a full scholarship and then went to vet school there. She's written a few books. I even saw her on C-SPAN once, talking about one of them. Something to do with mad cow disease."

"No shit."

The unknown girl was still talking to Lou, but Mr. Kray from next door had joined them. All Ronnie could see was the back of her head, but he could tell by the grins on the faces of both old men that she had to be pretty. He said, "Brenda Bergamo is a news anchor now in New York. I think it's an ABC affiliate." He could feel his control slipping, along with his co-ordination and his ability to speak clearly. He was revealing more than he would have if sober.

Gary popped a can. "I never asked before, but what did you do? I mean, did you scare 'em shitless with the story of Boneless Bernie?"

"Shit no, Gary. Jesus."

"I never heard of his ghost being seen around the place, but if I'd been you, I'd've used it. You'd think he'd haunt the place . . . You know what's weird? I've always thought of the guy as a lot older than me. But he was only seventeen when he died, so he never got older. Weird."

Ronnie nodded. He'd felt much the same, although he thought it would lower his dignity to agree with Gary too strongly.

Gary said, "Imagine falling so far that you turned every bone in your body to oatmeal."

"I'd rather not, thanks."

"No one ever figured out what he was doing up there."

Ronnie said, "Being a dumbass. Wasn't he drunk?"

"Yeah." Gary crushed the can in his meaty hand, and stared at the crumpled, sharpened edges of it as though there were coins somewhere inside. "I heard his brains were coming out his ears."

Dwelling on this image against his will, Ronnie said, "I don't know. I was, like, four years old. If that." He was doing his best to keep his squeamishness to himself. He couldn't tell how convincing he was being. He knew that Gary would run with it till they were both steeped in ghoulish stories and gross-out jokes, and Ronnie's stomach was feeling just delicate enough from the excess of beer that he knew this might ruin his afternoon.

He was on the verge of asking Gary about his kids just to change the subject, even though he was less interested in them than he was in Boneless Bernie, but then Gary asked, "So where the hell is Mary Galetti?"

Ronnie felt his surprise as anger, and said, "Shit, Gary, do you pay attention to anything but football?" Gary looked surprised, but Ronnie was committed to being irritated for the moment. "She was on the goddamn *space shuttle*. Three years ago. It was all over the goddamn news: *Pittsburgh's own Mary Galetti*. You know the way they do. She's some kind of scientist."

"Oh. No shit. You're right. I don't pay as much attention as I should to stuff like that." *Like at*. "But I'm not a hot-shit sports writer. I don't have an in with the papers and shit." Ronnie waited, knowing that Gary would take care of it for him, would take the blame, even though Ronnie had been the one out of line. Sure enough, Gary went on: "My dad gets my news for me. He watches all the news shit. The local channels anyway. The Channel 4 folks." He had a smile on his face now, a sickly one, drunk and ingratiating, and it made Ronnie feel lousy, so he took another drink. Gary added, "Those girls were behind me in school, so I never knew any of 'em, really. Except for Nia. But she never had anything to say to me, and that's not the kind of thing my dad knows about. C-SPAN and such."

"Yeah, well, I wouldn't follow it so much myself except . . ." He stopped himself, and covered by taking a drink. As he'd hoped, Gary took over for him again, still not grasping the important thing about these women.

"Except that you nailed all of 'em," Gary said, vicarious glee returning. "You nailed 'em by the light of the silvery atom smasher."

He was good and drunk by the time he could sever himself from Gary and join the rest of the party in the backyard. There were almost no children, which was refreshing, but which also made the gathering oddly sedate; in his youth, Memorial Day cookouts had teemed with them. Many of the same people were present, just grown up, and most of them were childless, one way or another. He saw Lou's daughter, his cousin Melissa, younger than him by four or five years, and waved her over. She'd always had a crush on him, or at least that was what Gary had told him a few summers ago. Ronnie had found the idea creepy, not only because of their blood tie, but because she had a jutting jaw, bad skin, and no breasts to speak of. She'd bred since then, so her breasts had more oomph to them now, but she was still homely. She greeted him with too much happiness, telling him that her three-year-old daughter was inside with the kid's father, a man from the city who Ronnie knew he'd met, but couldn't remember anything about. Ronnie made a slurred promise to say hello to them later, but managed to achieve his principle aim, which was to get information on the hot but faceless woman. Melissa said, "You mean Dana Asch? She just moved back in with her mom. Bad divorce. No kids." It didn't seem to occur to Melissa that she'd just described Ronnie's own situation. To his delight, Melissa hollered, "Dana! You met my cousin Ronnie? He's back now too."

She was older than he'd thought, maybe even over forty, but she looked great, the way a lot of movie stars manage to look perfect at forty, or even fifty, sometimes even hotter than they'd been at twenty. He didn't know what it was, maybe good bones or lucky genes. Probably just money, he thought. She looked like money too. Skin just tanned enough to look golden, hair just blond enough to look real, skin just taut enough to look like it was due to virtuous exercise, not plastic surgery. She smiled at him and his soberest thought was *Come to Papa.*

At first they chatted glibly by the grill, under the elated stare of Uncle Lou. They exchanged facts, some of which they already knew about each other. He learned that she'd gone to Pitt, then moved to San Francisco, gotten a job as a hospital administrator, married a doctor, and had lived in a large house with an ocean view. Neither mentioned divorce. She was enough older than he was that they didn't share many acquaintances, despite growing up in the same neighborhood. Then Mrs. Asch yelled, "Dana!" in an old-woman voice, and Dana gave a quick smile to Ronnie, then Lou, and moved away toward where her mother sat surrounded by three or four other elderly people in loud golf clothes. Yet he felt that some subtle consent had passed between them; he kept her in his peripheral vision, and when she walked into the house alone thirty minutes later, he followed her without anyone noticing.

She was in the kitchen, looking at a picture held by a strawberry-shaped magnet on the refrigerator door.

"My mother's black lab," Ronnie said. "Pepper. The dog's been dead for six years."

"That's sweet," she said.

She still looked good, even when he was quasi-sober. His head was finally clearing after all the beer he'd had with Gary, and he couldn't believe his luck. She turned to peer at him, and then her eyes broke away, darting around the room. His eyes followed hers, and he could see they were truly alone, if only for a moment. He turned back to her and then she leaned forward and kissed him on the mouth, quickly but hard, a serious kiss. She pulled back and stared at him with shining hazel eyes. She said, "No one can know. I'm 'going out with girlfriends' tonight. I just moved back. I don't want my mother to know anything."

He nodded, then asked, "Do you know the path to the atom smasher? Where it comes out by the ballfield?"

She smiled wide, almost laughing. "Oh my God. Yes." She dropped her voice. "Two hours from now. Bring wine. I'll bring cups. And watch out for poison ivy."

It was like a military maneuver through a jungle. It was only spring, so the milkweed and Virginia creeper weren't as thick as they would be in July or August. Still, the path was dark and a little muddy; if there hadn't been a tacit ban on speaking, he would have joked that they could use a machete. Here and there they passed wild raspberry bushes; he remembered that Mary Galetti had liked to eat the ripened berries on the way up the hill.

The hurricane fence was at the top of a rise, steep like all hillsides in the neighborhood. The fence was the same, which was a shock. Even the spot he'd most often used in the past hadn't been mended, where the green-painted metal knots only kissed the ground instead of digging deep into it. The fencing was even still bent in the same places. All it took was a hard jerk and the hole was big enough to scoot through. Nothing has changed, he thought. How weird is that? He'd brought pliers in his backpack, hoping they'd be enough to bend the wire fence to get in; he'd been praying that he wouldn't need his father's bolt cutters. There was simply no way he could have snuck them out of the house. Now it turned out that even the pliers were unnecessary.

She was behind him, no backpack of her own, just a plastic bag that she said held some Dixie cups and snacks. He didn't know if she'd brought condoms or not, but he had a pocketful. He'd never gotten anyone pregnant in his life that he knew of, and that was a good thing. At her age, he wasn't sure if she could even get pregnant. But since he didn't really know her, there was always the tiny possibility that she was worried about her biological clock, and saw him as a possible sperm donor. I just want my seed spilled where it won't do anything but lie there, he thought, realizing that the metaphor was a strange one, full of double entendres, and he almost laughed. The thought of disease didn't worry him at all.

Behind him, she said, "You're about to put your hand in a bunch of poison ivy." She was right; the three-pointed leaves quivered in the slight wind from his breath as he drew his hand back from the weak part of the fence. Her voice was quiet, but not a whisper; there didn't appear to be anyone else around. Careful to avoid the poison ivy, he pulled up on the fence, which bent obligingly up, till they could walk through if they stooped. He led the way, and then held the flap of wire fencing back for her. Once she was through he carefully put the fencing back in place, the way he always had. They stayed silent as they made their way across the parking lot, across asphalt so cracked and uneven it looked like an earthquake had stirred up the dirt underneath.

The night was fine and clear, with sharp, bright stars overhead and the red glow of the city just visible above the trees to the west. The entire vast parking lot could be seen with one turn of the head, and it was clear that they were alone. The only sounds were distant ones: the buzz of an air-conditioning unit outside the closest house; a motorcycle bursting loudly up to speed on Ardmore Boulevard, only two blocks away but remote over a tree-covered rise; firecrackers popping on a concrete driveway. All distant sounds, all benign.

He took her hand then, and looked her in the eye. Now was a critical time; he needed to make sure she continued to think this was fun, a romantic adventure they were sharing, not a sordid episode, which it could easily morph into if it wasn't handled with careful, experienced hands. He smiled, she smiled back, and he felt himself relax.

"Let's go up on the platform," he said in a soft voice. He pointed to the rusty metal steps that began in shadows at the base of the atom smasher, perched on the unlovely rectangle of corrugated steel and concrete.

"It's really big when you're right next to it," she whispered.

"Are you afraid of heights?" he asked.

"Not really. But I'm not a kid anymore, you know? I'm in pretty good shape, but still, all those stairs."

"They used to be pretty sturdy. Even if they've rusted more since I was here last, the metal was really thick. They should still be okay."

They made their way to the base of the stairs, and he put

out a hand to find where the railing started. It was rough with rust, and he waited until his eyes adjusted to the dimness and he could get a better look to see if the metal staircase had deteriorated in the decade since he'd last climbed it. It was too dark to see well, and although he had a flashlight, he didn't want to use it unless he had to; there was a good chance that it would be seen by neighbors if anyone was near a window. He shook the railing, but it didn't budge, so he put his foot on the first step. It too felt firm, and now his eyes were dark-adapted enough that he could see the sturdy gray outline of the staircase reaching up to the bulge of the dome. He went up two more steps, and then turned and reached his hand down to her. She took it.

There were two platforms: one at the widest part of the inverted pear shape of the atom smasher dome, and a smaller one at the very top, like a widow's walk. The steps ended halfway to the lower platform, replaced by a ladder; this too seemed in good shape, still firmly attached, and so the rest of the climb to the first platform was no harder than he remembered. After stepping off the ladder, he reached down for her hand and helped her the rest of the way onto the metal floor. Fortunately, it was a solid steel sheet and not grillwork, or he would never have had the success he'd had up here; no sleeping bag would have been thick enough to make it comfortable. The sinking of the sun had cooled the hills, and so they'd each changed clothes since the afternoon; both had on jeans and running shoes and long-sleeved shirts. Hers was black and plain, his was a Steelers jersey.

He pulled a blanket out of his backpack; it was the spare one kept in a box under his bed, so his mother wasn't likely to miss it, even if she went snooping. He spread the blanket over the metal floor of the platform and then reached into his pack again for the magnum of wine that he'd managed to cadge from the cookout. Dana pulled a handful of cloth hand-kerchiefs from her plastic grocery bag, whispering an apology that she was a "clean freak" and liked to be able to wipe off her hands. She put the handkerchiefs in her jeans pockets, and then produced two Dixie cups circled with little purple flowers from her plastic bag, separated them, and handed both to Ronnie. He unscrewed the bottle, joking about the fact that there was no cork. He filled a cup and handed it to her. When he had his own, they toasted silently, the cups making no sound as they touched.

"I think we're safe now," he said.

She laughed softly. "So what made you think of this place? Do you bring all the women you meet up here?"

He shook his head, taking another sip of the paper-flavored wine. "Only the special ones." He laughed too, feeling the air brush him, seeing the stars on the carpet of trees in the valley below them that were really the lights of the eastern suburbs, North Versailles and Turtle Creek. The exotic names of the not-very-exotic places that had created him. "The truth is, I haven't been up here in almost fifteen years. Not since my senior year in high school."

"Really? I guess I really am special."

He laughed again, not telling her that he hadn't been home enough since then for it to become an issue anyway. "Didn't you ever sneak in here? Maybe climb up to the top on a dare?"

"I don't take dares," she said. "Of course I've been here. Everyone comes here sooner or later. But not in a long, long time. And even when I was a kid, I believed all the stories about radiation."

He was about to mention the ghost of Boneless Bernie, but thought better of it. Her hair was still up in that cute bunchy ponytail, and he said, "I'd like to kiss you."

"I'd like to kiss you too," she replied. "But not yet."

He nodded and leaned back, resting against the curved metal behind him.

"Are you sure it's *not* still radioactive?" she aked.

"I have no idea," he said. "But I'm not interested in having kids, so I don't think it matters much."

"Still, you don't want to die young for a dumb reason like that—because you leaned against a building that happened to poison you."

"I think it's shielded," he said, although he didn't really know. "I can't believe they'd leave it just sitting here if it was spraying radiation all over the place."

"Well, they don't expect people to be up here rolling around in it." There was a smile in her voice, and he could tell she wasn't really worried, so he decided to change the subject.

"I'll tell you about my train wreck if you tell me about yours."

"What train wreck?"

He poured them each more wine, saying, "Both of us have just moved back in with our parents. I didn't do it because it made my life more worth living. I did it because I have to. I don't want to assume the same for you, but the odds are, you're not back home because it's your life's ambition either."

She laughed again, a lovely soft sound that revealed perfect teeth gleaming in the soft glow from the light on the street on the far side of the building behind them. It radiated around the huge metal structure like a shadow in reverse.

"He lost his medical license," she said. "Too many kickbacks from a couple of drug companies. A little Medicare fraud. He's in Tacoma now. I wasn't interested in following him."

"Man, that's cold," he said, smiling.

"Not as cold as living in a slum in San Francisco. What about you?"

"A similar story. But morally I didn't do anything wrong. No offense to your ex."

"You have my permission to offend him all you want."

"Thanks. I just lost my job. Downsizing. Fucking economy." He thought of Gary, then tried not to.

"To the fucking economy," she said, saying the latter word properly, and they toasted again. A warm breeze made a brown curl dance by her left ear as she added, "So how many girls have you brought up here, exactly?"

He paused, then thought, she'll laugh, but that's okay. "Eleven." He took a deep breath. The air was tinged with sulphur from the one remaining steel mill in Braddock, a few short miles away. He didn't remember when the mills had filled the landscape and clotted the sky with fire and smoke. But she might, he thought. The notion was startling. He said, "There's a thing about that. An interesting thing."

"What's that?" He again heard the smile in her voice. I'm going to do it with her, he thought. Right here, like old times. It won't be right away, but that's okay. One of the perks of being a grown-up is understanding the joys of delayed gratification.

"The interesting thing is about the girls. Every one of them had things happen to them after they were up here with me."

"What?" Her voice had a little sharpness to it, maybe of fear, and he realized how badly he'd said it; she didn't really know him and might think he meant something bad, so he hurried on. "No, no. I mean good things." He drained the cup and reached for the bottle. "Really good things. Like, they got rich suddenly, or their parents did. Or they got scholarships. Or they got into their first choice college, even if they didn't expect to." He looked at her, and she was looking back, but it was difficult to read her face even though his eyes could see pretty well now that they'd spent so much time in the dark. "It was every single time. They each got what they really wanted. One girl really wanted to be a cheerleader, and she got picked two weeks later, against some pretty big odds. Some of them, the good stuff happened a bit later on, but all of them, every single one, has had a great life ever since. So far, anyway. Every single one."

She was quiet for a moment, and he could feel his heart beating a little fast, and he waited with no idea what her reaction would be. Then she said, "You're helping me out, is that what you're saying?" And then she was laughing, and at first he was a little annoyed, even hurt, but then laughed with her as she added, "You're a good luck charm. That's so wonderful."

He put his arm around her shoulders, and she let him. He expected her to lay her head upon his, but instead, she took another drink, draining the Dixie cup, and then held it in front of him. He moved his arm away to give her another refill. The air cooled and began to move more around them, and there were gray clouds appearing here and there in the sky, small ones with rose bellies from the city far below. The ambient light caught her straight white teeth as she grinned at him; then she said, "That's amazing. Really amazing."

"I know," he said, relief clutching him, and he realized how tightly he'd held onto this truth about himself, a truth he'd never shared with anyone, even his wife. Of course, he'd never brought his wife up here. Now that she'd left him the moment the chips were down, he was glad. "I'm relieved that you don't think I'm nuts. You don't, do you?" He was feeling the wine now, feeling drunk for the second time that day, and he thought, I'd better slow down if I want everything to work later. He added, "It's occurred to me that it was lucky for me too, at least it was until recently, and I thought, well, if I'm going to be superstitious, might as well go all the way. Maybe it brought me luck too, by setting me on the right path, or something. And I sure could use being set on the right path again. So maybe we can both get something out of it." He thought, you're drunk, stop talking.

She shifted suddenly, startling him. She placed her hand on his shoulder and used it to support herself as she stood up. She rocked a little, and he realized that she was drunk as well. Her hand moved from his shoulder to the side of the atom smasher as she steadied herself. Then she pulled her hand away, looking at the spot where her hand had pressed against the metal as though expecting to see a print in the dim light.

"It's not radioactive," he said, although in truth he didn't know if there was any danger in touching the bare metal. He'd done it so many times in the past he couldn't imagine there being something poisonous about the place, but he knew nothing about radiation; he knew about sports, for Christ's sake, about batting averages and hat tricks and careers made by extraordinary feats of strength and coordination, and lost by torn sinews and addiction. Only not anymore. *You're just not that good.*

He stood up, steadying himself the same way she had, his hand on the warm curved metal. It's warm because it's been sitting in the sun all day, he thought. Not because its atoms are burning up.

"I want to go up," she said. "All the self-help books I've ever read say you have to take risks to get anywhere. You make your own luck. We'll be lucky for each other. Let's take a risk. Let's go up."

Two horizontal bars led from the platform to the bottom of the upper ladder; she grabbed the uppermost of these while stepping onto the lower one, and then she began to work her way left before Ronnie was fully on his feet. "Dana," he said, using her name for the first time, an image of her tumbling forty or so feet down onto broken asphalt in his unwilling mind, maybe her brains coming out of her ears. She ignored him and moved onto the ladder without losing her grip while Ronnie looked on with growing dismay. Then she started climbing, slowly at first, then more quickly when the ladder turned into steps as it curved toward the top. There were handrails on either side which she touched only lightly, as though she didn't want to get her hands any dirtier than she had to. When she was partially out of sight, she paused and turned slightly to look down at him, her body only a black silhouette against the pink and gray sky. The wind was blowing harder now, and her hair began to wave at him from the confines of its wild ponytail. "Come on, Ronnie," she called softly, the wind carrying her voice away from him. "Be my good luck charm."

And so he grabbed the horizontal rails, grateful that he didn't have a fear of heights even when sober, although he knew that if he looked down or thought too much about what he was doing, that might change. He crab walked until he reached the ladder, only maybe fifteen feet away, then shifted his weight onto the ladder itself, deeply relieved that it seemed to be solid. It only creaked a little when it took on the weight of his whole body, and so he started to believe that neither of them was going to follow the flight path of Boneless Bernie. Ronnie moved up and up, beyond the point where the ladder curved into steps as it leveled off; the change was disorienting, making it tricky to find his center of balance, but he kept going until at last he was at the top.

The platform at the summit was little more than a crow's nest with just enough room for two people to stand comfortably. It was protected by a waist-high metal railing, and she was gripping it with both hands, her back to the edge, facing him, so when he was able to stand free of the steps, slightly winded, he was only inches from her. He knew the view was spectacular; when he was young he tended to stay below when he brought company because of the lack of room up here, and even at night the cops could easily see you at the top if they were looking. But he had loved it, he remembered now, had loved creeping up here by himself on the occasional night when he was alone, or with a girl who was particularly daring. He never stayed long, and the climb had always been scary, but it had been worth it.

Dana let go of the railing, put her arms around his waist, and kissed him deeply on the mouth, her tongue caressing his teeth. Then she pulled her tongue out, sucking his into her with a wine-soaked fierceness that aroused him in a way he hadn't known since adolescence.

She pulled back and laughed so softly that the wind carried it away altogether; he couldn't hear it but could feel it radiating off her; it only made her more magnetic, more hot, more sexually necessary to him.

She said, "This place was my good luck charm too." He could just make her voice out in the wind that blew the stars around over their heads. "Maybe it wasn't you, Ronnie. Maybe it was the place itself." She turned around, pushing her hips against the railing, and he pressed himself into her back, pressed himself in her ass, into the backs of her thighs. "Ronnie, I never thought about it before," she was saying, "but you were right. Everything good for me started here." Her body rubbed against his as she turned around, facing him again, and she had a handkerchief in her hand, and all he could think of was a handjob where she needed something to keep herself from getting all sticky. He could smell her warm, Merlot-infused breath as she said into his mouth, "I thought it was just an accident. Bad luck. But it was like a sacrifice or something. It's been twenty-one years. Is that a significant number?" She laughed and Ronnie tried to understand what she was saying. "Maybe twenty years is the limit," she continued. "I didn't mean for anything to happen, but maybe that's why everything went so well after that. I got everything I wanted."

And then Ronnie realized that she was talking about Boneless Bernie, and he felt her hands, like pistons on his chest, two blows so hard they hurt, and who would expect a woman to be so strong she could hurt you like that? And then he felt like he was swimming, only it was through air instead of water. He hit something that felt sharp like a gunshot, and then he was free again, falling, and it was like a carnival ride that you know is a terrible mistake as soon as it starts moving, but you can't get off no matter what, and even through the dark he could see her, so far up, blowing him a kiss, and already wiping down the railing at the top of the giant inverted teardrop, before he met the broken asphalt.

STILL AIR

East Liberty

The morning after Amp got killed our neighborhood was lit up with rumors. My mother and me, we barely even made the block before someone passing said, almost with a whistle, "You hear that nigga Amp got popped by some gangbangers?" Someone else said, carrying the news like a bag of bricks, "Sad what happened to that boy who got robbed last night." People who didn't know Amp or his kin said, "I know his mother." "I knew his pops." Rumors idled in the slow drag of the traffic, the rich Fox Chapellers and Aspinwallers who drove across the Allegheny River into what was our little moat of trouble: Penn Circle, the road looping East Liberty like a noose.

Lies, gossip, bullshit, half-truths spread out, carried in the school and city buses. Pompano heard it was two white guys, probably plainclothes cops, that took Amp out. Walking by with her girlfriends, Shelia said she heard gunshots and shouts. "Amp went out shooting shit up like a true thug," she cackled, pointing her finger at me like the barrel of a gun. Her girlfriends laughed like she wasn't talking about someone who'd actually been killed. I mean, Amp was dead and people was already kicking his name around like it never had any air inside it.

This is why I never wanted anybody to give me a nickname. Well, that ain't exactly true. Most people call me De-

mario, but I used to let Star call me Fish sometimes. My grandmother used to call me Fish. Her "little fish," even though I
was taller than her by the time I was fourteen. I didn't even
know Amp's real name. Maybe I heard a teacher say it when
we was in preschool at Dilworth. *Anthony Tucker. Andrew
Trotter.* By first grade the teachers, even Principal Paul with
her thick-assed eyeglasses and that belt squeezed too tight
around her gray pantsuit, called Amp "Amp." It was the only
name he answered to.

I can't really say he was my friend, though, to tell you the
truth. He was never really in class that much, and then he
dropped out of high school junior year. Star said it was because he wanted to get a job as soon as he heard she was pregnant, but I think he'd have dropped out anyway. He spent his
days on the corner behind Stanton Pharmacy. He was always
there in jeans so new it looked like he hadn't even washed
them yet. New sneakers, pro jerseys—people said he had a
Steelers jersey for damn near every player. You'd think he'd be
there waving his shit in my face or calling me a clown, but I
don't think he ever even noticed me. He'd look right through
me, call me *youngblood* even though we were the same age.

And once he sold me a hammer, I shit you not. It was in
the book bag on my shoulders that morning. Even crazier, he
sold my mother a big twenty-four-inch level. How he got her
to buy it, I'll never know. But that's what he did—or what
he'd been doing for the last couple of months. Word was out
and people, mostly old dudes trying to make ends doing handy
work or whatever in Highland Park, would buy shit from him.
He'd take you around the corner to a grocery cart full of stuff.
I saw he had a cordless drill and a circular saw one day. An
empty paint bucket and a couple of utility knives the next. I
bought the hammer for two dollars. It was big too. Practically

a mallet. I doubt Amp kept what he didn't sell. He just wanted to get paid. Rumor was, he was stealing things from Home Depot, but I saw the shit. Most of it was used. None of it was useless but most of it was used.

You'd find him near Stanton Pharmacy with that dog that always followed him around, some scrawny watered-down pit bull he called Strayhorn. The dog always barked at me. It'd go to barking like it wanted to bite me in my kneecaps when I passed and wouldn't stop until I was down the street. For a long time I thought Amp was whispering *sickems* in the dog's dull gray ears, but now I think he was just talking all kinds of mysterious shit to it. That's why Star liked him. Why she dumped me for him, I guess. She said he had poetry in him.

"I heard they killed the boy's dog too!" my mother said to her friend Miss Jean as we stood waiting for the 71A. This is what I tried to do every morning: walk my mother to her bus. It was the only time we got to talk since I was usually knocked out by the time she came home from work in the hospital kitchen. I know it sounds like I'm some kind of momma's boy or that I'm soft-hearted, but it was something my grand-mother made me promise to do. In fact, I only started calling my mother "Mother," instead of "Marie" like I used to, after my grandmother died. I used to call my grandmother "Mother" and my mother "Marie," because when we all lived together in the East Mall projects, that's what I heard them call each other. You remember the East Mall? The damn building used to straddle Penn Avenue, cars drove right beneath it. Now that that shit's been demolished, I almost can't believe we lived there. I mean, who puts a building right on top of the street? If Penn Circle was the moat, well, the East Mall was like one of its bankrupt castles. No, better yet, it was like an old drawbridge that couldn't be lowered. Anyway, we were on the fifth floor so I never heard any actual traffic, but when I looked out of my window, I could see the cars going and coming 24/7. I could see the houses in four neighborhoods at once: Shadyside, Friendship, East Liberty, I could see where Penn Avenue curved up the hill to Garfield.

If I had a better sense of Pittsburgh history, I could tell you all the stuff my grandmother used to tell me. I mean in detail. When the civic arena was built in the '50s, I think it was the '50s, a lot of blacks were driven from their homes in the Hill District. Some ended up in Homewood or on the North Side, some moved out this way. My grandmother could also tell you, gladly, about all the famous Pittsburgh Negroes from back in the day. Mary Lou Williams. George Benson. And Billy Eckstine, who grew up just a few blocks away in Highland Park. She would sing "Skylark," which is a song I think he must have made. If she had the record she would have played it all the time, no doubt. *Skylark, have you anything to say to me? Won't you tell me where my love can be? Is there a meadow in the mist, where someone's waiting to be kissed?* It went something like that.

"Yep. They killed the boy and his dog, I can't believe it," my mother said this time, bothering a white man with his dress shirt cuffs rolled up to his hairy forearms. He didn't have a single tattoo.

East Liberty had been plush once, that's what my grandmother always said. Decorated with big unvandalized houses. But then they dropped a lasso on the neighborhood in the late '60s. Homeowners moved across town and contracted their shabby cousins and uncles to convert their old places into shabby rental units. The living rooms were the size of bedrooms, the bedrooms the size of closets. Businesses left, the projects came. You know that little strip of Highland Park

Avenue between Centre and East Liberty Boulevard that cuts through Penn Circle like the white line on a *DO NOT ENTER* sign? My grandmother hated it, but that's where everybody hung out. The blackest block for blocks. After they demolished all the projects and got a Whole Foods and Home Depot and a fancy bookstore, white people started calling it the East End. Fucking changed the name of the part of the neighborhood they wanted back. We still call it Sliberty, though.

My grandmother said the neighborhood was on white people's minds again. White people young enough to be the grown children of the people who'd left decades ago. Contractors were called to make the apartments houses again. They'd be corralling us like a bunch of Indians, my grandmother said. She said "Native Americans" but I knew what she was talking about. Reservations and Indian-giving and shit. I rarely heard her call people their real names. I once heard her ask this Mexican lady if she preferred "Latino" or "Hispanic." And sometimes, when she was being sarcastic, she might say "Negro," but I never heard her used the word "nigga." She said things like: "Look at these Negroes." The way she said it sounded worse than "nigga" to me. She was dead with cancer before she had a chance to see me and Marie living on our own for the first time.

"They ain't kill his dog, it wasn't that kind of thing," someone said behind me. It was Benny giving me the *wuzzup* nod and then flipping open his cell phone.

"People saying it was some plainclothes white cops, but I know it wasn't cops," I said to him.

"No, I heard it wasn't cops too, yo," he replied, assuming I'd heard it from the same place he had.

"Pranda said they was some old country-looking motherfuckers. Some old long-hair-and-plaid-vests shit. She was 'bout to call the cops about it, but I was like, *Them motherfuck-ers ain't even been caught yet! They find out you been talking to the PoPo, they coming for you.*" He shook his head while holding the cell phone to his ear. I couldn't tell if he was talking to me or the person on the other line. "I think they were drug deal-ers from down south," he said. "Some old meth heads or some shit. Naw, man, fuck no. I ain't going back over that bitch house until them motherfuckers get caught!" He laughed into the phone.

Marie. My mom, her bus showed up either just ahead of schedule or just behind it, depending on your perspective. It was never on time. She never said anything like, "Home right after school." She knew I'd be there. Homework done. Learn-ing more from television than I ever did at school. She kissed me on my face the same way her mother used to kiss me and her. Then she'd whisper, "My little fish." I pretended I didn't hear it. Told her, "Goodbye. Be good."

I was supposed to walk to school, get there five or ten minutes before the first bell. But I was going to see Amp's people. His uncle Shag would want to know what I knew. Or I should say, if Shag heard I knew anything, I should see him be-fore he sent someone to find me. Everybody said he was kind of crazy. He didn't sell drugs or anything, but he'd been in jail a few years for something. Nobody fucked with him.

I wanted to tell Shag what I knew, but first I went back to the alley where, the night before, I'd seen Amp running with the white men right behind him. There was a big old dump-ster there. I let my hand rest for a moment on its lid before I opened it and looked inside. The smell crawled over my face. Black garbage bags, white garbage bags, little tiny plastic bags, muddy liquid rot, an old sneaker, a lawn chair—it was all sour.

But there was no corpse. No dog, no tatt-covered body. Amp had tattoos all along his neck and arms. On the back of each of his hands was his dad's name and R.I.P in block letters. As if the man had died twice. Or as if Amp might forget him in the time it took him to look from one hand to the other. I heard he got Star's name tattooed over his heart as soon as she got pregnant, but I don't think that shit was true.

When I got to Amp's house nobody was there. I guess they could have been at the morgue. People said they'd seen the ambulance, the body bag. Everybody noticed when an ambulance or police cars blazed through the neighborhood. I pulled out my phone and looked down the block. New houses were being built along the streets I had passed walking to Amp's. They stood out like new cars in a junkyard next to the dumps around them. They were big odd-colored places. Light green, light blue, light red wood siding. They looked like empty dollhouses, even the one or two that actually had white people living inside. The FOR SALE signs called them Historic District houses and had prices with six digits. Like whoever was selling them wanted us to know we could never afford them. More old houses were being leveled and more new "historic" houses were being built on top of them. Construction workers, real estate agents, young families, white people were coming and going through the neighborhood's side streets. It wasn't a big deal. Nobody was scary or threatening or anything. Sometimes we'd wave when they passed us on the street.

And anyway, most of the guys I knew were truly minor criminals. Burglarizing the cars and backyards of Highland Park for chump change. No one who was really hardcore lasted long. Not because they got killed in a drive-by or something you see in a movie, though that happened occasionally, but because they usually got snatched by the police before they could do anything that was truly gangster. Everyone was happy when Chuck Ferry was off the streets, for example. He was just too dangerous for anybody's good. The streets were left more often than not to a mix of loiterers, dudes like Amp, and tired old men and boys who did little more than strut along the corners and back alleys. But when I passed them the morning after Amp was killed, everybody seemed nervous. I could feel it. Everybody was anxious to have the villains off the street so the neighborhood could be returned to itself.

"Heard ya boy got got," a dude said when he saw me sitting on Amp's steps. He was a few years older than me. I knew he was looking for some little bit of gossip he could take with him on down the road.

"Wasn't my boy," I said without looking him in the eye.

"Damn. That's some cold shit to say, youngblood." The dude stared until I looked at him. Then walked off with something like mild disgust flickering across on his face.

I've never been in a fight. I've never even broke up a fight. I'm the quiet dude that's always watching from the edge of the clash. Dude like me, always the first one people ask what happened. "You saw that shit, Demario? Who threw the first punch?" Usually I know, but I don't say. The conversations go faster that way. I got no problem with bystanding. One time Star sort of hinted that was my problem. I didn't think it was a put down at first.

Star. She is without a doubt the blackest person I know. Which is funny because she is also yellow as a brown banana. She didn't wear dashikis and all that Back-to-Africa shit, but she wore these white shells in her braids. And she knew everything there was to know about Malcolm X, M.L.K., W.E.B. Them famous Negroes whose names were initials. She still had an *OBAMA 08* sign propped up in her bedroom window. I could see it whenever I stood across the street looking at her house. I never got, you know, to run my hands over her body and all that, but I know she had a little tattoo shaped like Africa somewhere under her clothes. She never showed it to me.

"What you doing?" I said with a flatness I meant to sound cool when I phoned her. I knew she wouldn't be at school. She was like eight months pregnant. She'd have the baby in a couple of weeks and be back to finish the last two months of our junior year at Peabody.

"I can't talk to you right now, Mario."

"Yeah, I know. I heard what happened to Amp."

She was quiet. Like she was holding her breath. I knew she'd been crying. After a long minute, she said, "I just don't know why this is happening." Damn. Then we were quiet a little while longer.

"I saw the dudes."

"Who? You saw the dudes that did it?"

"Don't worry, I'm gonna take care of it for you."

"Who'd you see?"

Amp wasn't dead yet when I saw him, I almost told her. I thought of how they had him pinned to a dumpster in an alley off Black Street. Two wiry, scruffy men. The dog, Strayhorn, was snapping at the pant leg of one of them. The guy gave the dog a frantic kick and then kicked at Amp in the same frantic way. They sort of snatched and poked at him. Amp's shirt had been ripped. He was bleeding. I could hear him saying, "I ain't got your shit. I ain't got your shit." Declaring it, really. Like he wasn't afraid. Like he was in charge even if they were the ones grabbing and shoving and delivering awkward blows. They could barely handle him. I knew they weren't gangsters. But I still did nothing.

"I'm gonna take care of this shit," I said to Star, half talking up my nerve. I didn't really know what I was saying.

"Don't go trying to be a hero, Mario."

"No, it ain't like that."

"Just go to the police."

"Police?"

"Or go by his house— Wait a minute," she said, putting me on hold.

I rubbed my brow. I thought for the first time that calling the police wasn't such a bad idea. I won't say I had plans to take care of Star, exactly. All the money I made working at the Eagle went to Marie. We lived in this little-ass apartment. My mother had been strange since her mother died. She was working long, lonely hours. She was my priority. And then Amp's death last night, well, I told you she kissed me like her mother used to: a peck on each cheek then on my nose. Shit was embarrassing. I jerked back just a bit, but then I relaxed. I knew she was sad.

The phone clicked back on: "Demario?"

"Yeah? Why you put me on hold?"

"Listen: go over to Amp's house and tell his uncle what you saw."

"I'm there now. Ain't nobody here."

"You there now? At Amp's house?"

"Yeah," I said. "Fuck is wrong with you, Star?"

"Don't cuss at me," she said.

"I want to see you."

She sighed. "No. You can't see me."

"I'm coming by."

"Just stay there. Wait for Shag . . . Come by after you speak to him."

So that's what I did. I sat on the steps with my hands

in my pockets. Had there been no baby, maybe Star would have gotten back with me. Had there been no baby and no Amp, maybe she could have let herself fall for me. I ain't bad looking. Amp was just a little taller. But he had these long dreadlocks, where I just have this little nappy afro. Not even enough to braid into cornrows. Once when we were hanging out at Highland Park, Star said she liked my Asiatic Black Man eyes. She grabbed my jaw and looked right into them like she was reading something. Fuck, I hadn't ever heard the word *Asiatic* before.

People thought my grandmother had some Asian in her. She had a pudgy face—before the cancer got at her—she had a pudgy face and these slanted eyes that made her look like she was just waking up. If you were on her bad side her face looked full of NotToBeFuckedWithness. I know dudes who just moved and nodded when they saw her walking their way. But if you were on her good side, the same face, the same expression, just seemed real mellow. She'd nod back to those brothers almost without moving her head. She really wasn't to be fucked with, though, that's for sure. She kept a fat switchblade in her bra. I got it now.

After thirty, forty minutes, Shag pulled up in an old gray sedan. He was a long skinny man. Going bald. He almost didn't have to lean over to roll down the passenger-side window.

"Who are you, boy? What you want?" He didn't seem all that fucked up over anything. Just suspicious as anyone who finds somebody on his porch in the middle of the day.

"I'm Demario. I used to go to school with your nephew Amp."

Shag didn't exit the car. I started thinking he wasn't as calm as I first thought. Seemed like he was figuring something out. Maybe he thought I had a gun or something. All I had was a few books and a hammer in my backpack. And my grandmother's blade. I had that in my back pocket.

"I saw what happened to him last night," I told Shag.

People were saying the dudes who'd killed Amp hadn't been caught, that was true for the moment. People were saying some sort of drug shit was involved, it didn't seem like that to me. I'd seen them but the stupid dog was the only one to notice me. He barked with the gray hair up on his neck. But it wasn't his usual wild, territorial bark. There was urgency in it. Fear. I probably imagined it. The whole thing couldn't have taken more than a minute or two.

I cleared my throat. "I think it was a couple of dudes who been renovating those houses on Euclid."

That was my theory. It should have felt good to tell him, but it didn't.

"Come here," he said, waving me to the car window. He glanced up and down the street in a way that made me nervous. But what else could I do? Couldn't run with him right there looking at me. I walked over to him with my hand stuffed in my pockets.

"What they do with him? You tell the cops?"

"I don't know what they did. That's why I came over. See how he doing." That was mostly true. I'd come hoping Amp was alive, hoping the rumors were lies. But really, I just didn't want Shag to ask why I hadn't helped his nephew survive. I'd seen Amp fighting back. The dog was barking at me. Like it was saying, *They're gonna kill him, they're gonna kill him, do something!* Amp broke free, running off into the darkness of the alley with the men behind him. Maybe his dog barked at me just a beat longer before it realized I wasn't going to do anything. It turned, running after them. I didn't follow.

"Well, he ain't here . . ." Shag said, getting out of the car.

"Okay." I could see it in his face, he was lying to see if I'd know he was lying.

"You should come in with me and wait for him, he'll be back soon probably," Shag said.

"No, I got some errands to run. I might come back by later."

Shag chuckled slightly and said, half to himself, "Nigga talking about *errands*." He was jingling his keys.

"I'll come back later."

"Man, come on in the house," he said. Then, a little bit softer: "I got something I want you to do."

"Amp ain't alive is he?" I said. Blurted.

"No, he ain't," he sighed. "He ain't."

He opened the door and I followed him up a flight of stairs to the second floor where he and Amp and Amp's mother lived. I don't know where she was. Bawling at the East Liberty precinct. Picking out caskets. I thought the air smelled funny. Damp, salty with grief maybe. She might have been locked in her bedroom dreaming her son was still alive. We moved down a tiny hallway to a tiny den. I recognized Amp in the wood-colored face of a boy on an end table. His first or second grade school portrait. His grin was so wide it showed every one of his teeth. He had a small gold stud in his ear. I remembered he'd been the first of the boys our age to get pierced. Instead of the white-collared shirts we were supposed to wear for our school uniforms at Dilworth, he wore a loose white T-shirt.

"Amp did that shit," Shag told me, pointing to where the thick blue carpet was yanked back revealing a perfect hardwood floor beneath it. "Told his momma he was going to fix this place up with his tools." Shag sat down on a plaid sofa that took up nearly all the space in the room. I saw the edge of a bedsheet spilling beneath it and figured it was where he slept.

"You want to smoke," he asked, pulling out a sandwich bag full of weed. He was settling in, I hadn't sat down yet.

"No," I said. Though I wanted to get high, really. What I really wanted was something to lift me from the ground. Up through the roof, up on above Penn Circle sitting like a bull's-eye in the middle of our neighborhood. Up on out of Pittsburgh. But I told him no and watched him roll a blunt.

"I told that nigga he was gone get jacked up for stealing them boys' shit," Shag said. He told me to sit down, but he didn't seem to care when I didn't. "I told his momma too. His room's full of their shit. Some dusty safety goggles, screwdrivers, dirty work gloves, dirty work boots, a fucking sliding T-bevel. You know what a T-bevel is? Amp didn't know either, but he got one in there."

Shag's phone buzzed on his hip but he didn't answer it.

"So I need you to do me a favor, youngblood. We need to ride over to where them motherfuckers are working and I need you to point them out to me."

"I didn't get a good look at them."

"That's all right. I want you to try. Just point in the right direction, know what I mean?"

He reached between the cushions of the sofa. I saw the butt of the gun just as his phone started buzzing again. This time he answered it. He smiled at me, then stood and walked from the room.

I sat down on the couch and touched the gun handle where it stuck out like the horn of an animal. I thought for a second about taking it and the bag of weed. Instead I got up, tipped to the hall, and listened. I could see into Amp's room. There were a pair of sneakers and a dog leash on his bed.

"No, I'll probably head to Newark. Atlanta. Somewhere with more black people than there are here." I could hear

Shag taking a piss in the bathroom while he talked. "You ain't good for shit, you know that, right? No. No, nigga, just stay there. I got somebody here gonna ride over there with me."

I thought again of the gun. Shag would want me to drive while he shot from the window. Or worse, he'd drive while he made me shoot. Either way, what I'd seen meant I'd have to be a part of what was going to happen.

I tried to be quiet running out of the house. I kept thinking I could hear a dog barking behind me. Amp's dog. The ghost of his dog. I didn't look back until I was panting around the corner. I was a few blocks from Star's house. But I turned toward Euclid where the new houses were being built.

There was a young white woman working in her yard. Planting flowers or something. Trimming the hedges. She glanced at me, then stared as I walked up the steps of the big empty house standing next to hers. There was no one there. I rattled the doorknob looking through its window into the wide bare rooms. I glanced back at the white woman who was pulling off her gardening gloves and still watching me. I pulled the hammer Amp sold me from my book bag and used it to smash the window on the door. The woman rushed inside her house. I reached through and tried to grab the door latch, but couldn't. I walked across the porch and hammered at the pane of the living room window until it broke open like a mouth with its teeth knocked out. It was loud as hell. I didn't fucking care. I guess I got cut. My blood dripping on the shiny hardwood floors almost looked like a trail of pennies.

I wanted to carve Amp's name somewhere no one would find it. Not for another fifty years or so. Not until the house had been lived in by rich white people, then rented out to poor black people, then renovated for white people again. I wanted someone in the future to strip back the sheetrock and find Amp's named carved into a beam. There was nowhere to carve it, though. Nowhere discreet. The kitchen didn't have cabinets yet. The bathroom on the first floor had no toilet. Wires hung from the ceilings and walls. Just an empty house. My grandmother said—she used to say this all the time—that people, black or white, would always fight over dirt but nobody could ever really own it. She said the land could only belong to the land. The rivers belonged to the rivers. The air was still air no matter who claimed to own it.

On the second floor I stood at a window in the master bedroom. Brick and sky, metal and wood, concrete and dirt, you already know what I saw out there: all the shit that gives air something to lean on. I knew the cops were on their way. And I'd have to do something. Say something. I thought I could already hear the sirens. I thought I could hear dogs trying to match the sound. I sat in the middle of the floor with the hammer in my lap. I had blood on my shirt and pants. I wasn't crying. I was barely breathing.

When I dialed Star's number, the dial tones echoed around me. We'd talked on the phone, but I hadn't seen her in weeks. Wasn't that I was afraid of Amp or his fucking dog. I just kept thinking she'd ask me over eventually. Soon as Amp fucked up, I figured she'd want to see me. And really, when I heard he was dead, I thought it was a reason to see her. Pregnant or not. I was going to be there for her. I was going to be with her.

Star didn't speak a word when she answered. "Hey," I said after a few seconds. I said it just as I'd said it to my mother when we came home from my grandmother's funeral. Sort of like it was a question. Softly. Slowly. It embarrassed me the same way when I said it then. "Hey."

DUPLEX

BY STEWART O'NAN

Bloomfield

She thought when Evelyn died she might finally get the second floor. She was not a selfish woman—a mother, a grandmother, used to doing for others—but in this one instance, after more than forty years of dealing with the soot and the street noise and people creeping through the alley and peeping in her windows, Anna Lucia felt she'd earned her reward.

She expected Eddie would leave and find his own place rather than live surrounded by his mother's old furniture. He was a dwarf and a drinker. He'd retired on full disability from the public works, and Evelyn had left him everything. Anna Lucia figured he'd take the money and buy one of those new condos over by Highland, since he spent most of his time in the bars along Penn anyway. Instead, a couple of months later he brought home a girlfriend twice his size and half his age.

She was last-call trash, a tall blonde, but ugly, a big-nosed Russian, right off the boat, like a mail-order bride who'd bailed at her first chance. Eddie had ruined his back in the sewers. He was paunchy and bald, hardly a catch. As far as Anna Lucia could tell, the girl didn't work.

Didn't cook either. Every night while Anna Lucia was fixing dinner for herself, they came clumping down, banging the outside door shut. She watched from her front window, frowning as he waddled to the car and held the passenger door for the girl, as if she was a lady. As if he was in love.

If so, that was even sadder. In the hospital, Evelyn had asked Anna Lucia to watch over him. She'd done her best, but Eddie was a grown man, and after all his problems, he deserved some happiness, even the fleeting kind.

Suddenly acquiring a new neighbor after having lived there alone for most of her adult life confused Anna Lucia. Out of shame, maybe, Eddie didn't introduce her. It was only by surprising them one evening on their way out that she learned the girl's name: Svetlana.

"Pliz to mit you," the girl said, shaking hands like a man.

She was taller than Dominic, with pitted cheeks and too much blush and her things falling out of her top. Not in a million years would Anna Lucia have let Roseanne leave the house like that, but Eddie seemed happy, dressed up like they were going somewhere fancy, and Anna Lucia was left to wonder exactly where as she picked at her leftovers.

They came back after the bars closed, laughing and making a racket on the stairs. Under the covers, she heard them moving from room to room, listened awhile, then settled back to sleep.

Some nights that was the end of it, but some nights they fought—no surprise, given their condition—and deep into the morning she woke to shouting and something heavy being knocked over, something being broken. Like most of the old row houses on the block, this one was brick, with plaster walls and high ceilings, so she couldn't make sense of what they were saying, only bursts of words that shocked her heart. She clamped her extra pillow to her ear, picturing the two of them squared off in Evelyn's living room, trading threats and accusations, destroying her precious snow globes and commemorative plates to make a point.

When their fights went on longer than Anna Lucia thought she could bear—when they sounded as if they were scuffling directly above her—she debated whether or not to call the police. She kept the phone Roseanne had given her on her nightstand. It would take so little. All she had to do was punch three numbers, yet every night, no matter how bad it sounded, she held off, not only because she suspected nothing would happen, but because they'd know it was her.

The mornings after these battles, she staked out the staircase, hoping to witness the damage—a puffy eye, a split lip—as if to prove she hadn't imagined the night before. Rarely was anything visible. Once, Eddie came down with a large gauze square taped to the side of his neck, maybe covering a scratch or a bite mark. The girl appeared untouched, though it was hard to say, with her long sleeves and all that makeup. They acted like everything was hunky-dory.

"Good mornink, Mizziz Nardinny."

"Good mor-ning, Svetlana," Anna Lucia enunciated. "How are you liking Pittsburgh?"

"I like Pizz-burr very much."

"Well, you couldn't ask for a better person to show you the city. He knows it inside out—literally."

"Ha, nice one, Mrs. N.," Eddie said, herding the girl toward the door.

"Have fun," Anna Lucia called after them, then stood there at the bottom of the stairs, biting the inside of her cheek, listening for his car to start.

She'd been waiting for this chance, but still wasn't sure. Her plan was to take the spare key Evelyn had given her and go up and see what condition the place was in. Right after Evelyn died, Anna Lucia had been a frequent visitor, carrying up a pan of lasagne or some tomatoes from the Tomassos' garden, but since the girl moved in, Eddie always stopped Anna Lucia at the door as if he was hiding something.

The key was in her little china teapot in the kitchen cupboard, along with her bingo money. All she needed was five minutes. She put the chain on the outside door for insurance and hurried up the stairs.

The place stank of cigarettes and old bacon grease. They'd rearranged everything. In the living room, on the antique sideboard where Evelyn had kept her family pictures, was a flat-screen TV. It faced her green velvet couch, covered with a flowered sheet spotted with burn marks. On the coffee table, beside a chipped glass ashtray piled with butts, as if waiting for their return, stood a half-full bottle of whiskey. Though her first instinct was to pour it down the sink, she made a point of not touching anything, kept silent as if someone might be listening.

The rug hadn't been vacuumed in ages. The kitchen floor was sticky, the counter crowded with glasses. Her plants were dry and dying. At least Eddie had left Evelyn's room alone— here were her snow globes and plates, exiled but safe—though he obviously never dusted. The bed in his room was mussed, a pair of pink sweatpants with JUICY written across the bottom draped over the headboard.

As she turned to leave, she noticed some money on his dresser—a wad of twenties folded in half, as if waiting to go into a wallet. She wondered if he was really that trusting or if he'd left it sitting out as a test. Whichever, it seemed wrong— like the girl's sweatpants, a taunt to all that was decent—and with her lips pinched in concentration, she stepped to the dresser, peeled two twenties from the wad, and slipped them into her pocket.

It was only after she added the bills to her teapot that she remembered to take the chain off.

She didn't say anything to Roseanne over the phone about her little visit, just let her know their fighting was getting worse.

"You want to hear fighting, you should hear Frankie and me going at it over the stupid insurance. People fight. Whatever it is, it's their business, not yours."

"They *drink* and they fight. It's different."

"Ma, listen to what you're telling me. Drunk people fight. That's not news."

"You're telling me I should have to listen to it every night?"

"I'm telling you it's what people do. It doesn't matter if they're big or small, black or white, Russian or whatever."

"I worry about Eddie."

"That's good of you, Ma, but it sounds like Eddie's doing what he wants to do."

"It's not right."

"Yeah, well, there's a lot of things in the world that aren't right, like the insurance companies, but we're not going to change them either."

"I'm just telling you, I'm not happy about it."

"Oh my God, will you stop?" Roseanne said. "Your complaint is registered."

That night they came home late, stumbling up the stairs. In bed she waited for them to begin. She tried to justify taking the money, telling herself it was for his own good, that Evelyn would want the girl out of her house. Anna Lucia had resolved to call the police once they got started, but after what seemed an endless silence—had they passed out?—instead of shouting and banging, she heard their footsteps cross the ceiling to his bedroom, and then that other, even more unwelcome noise she didn't want to picture.

The next night while they were out, she chained the door

again and took three twenties, leaving six, and then, seeing an opportunity, tore off the last of the toilet paper so there was just a thin square hanging from the roll.

It was a Friday, and they were later and louder than usual. They were already fighting out in the street. They continued the argument in the hall and then above her, the normal back-and-forth. There was no point calling the police until things got physical, and she lay in bed, staring up at the ceiling as if they might come falling through, until, after a long lull, finally there was a rumble of someone—maybe both of them—running, then yelling, and glass breaking, bottles possibly, china, and a thunderous crash that sounded like a dresser going over. Yes, that was what she'd been waiting for. Another crash, and then something smashing, maybe a plate. Someone or something big fell. She sat up and turned on her light, reached for her glasses and then the phone. The girl was screaming—keening, not making words at all—as Anna Lucia punched the buttons and calmly gave the dispatcher her address.

Waiting for the police, she heard someone coming down the stairs, and rushed to the front window in time to see the girl hustle between the parked cars and across the street with a duffel bag. Anna Lucia couldn't be sure it was her plan that had worked, but in any case she was grateful. She thought Evelyn would be too.

Upstairs there was no sound. She considered going up, but it was three in the morning and Eddie might not want to see her. She sat by her front window, watching from behind the blinds as the police arrived with their lights going.

They rang the bell, then banged on the door. After a time, Anna Lucia went out with one hand holding her robe closed at her neck and let them in.

"You the complainant?" the big one asked.

"They're fighting again." She pointed and stood there as they climbed the stairs.

A couple minutes later the short one came down. His forehead was sweating. "You said 'they're fighting.' Who's 'they'?"

She told him about Eddie. No, she didn't know the girl's last name.

"Any idea where she might be?"

"She ran off toward Liberty right after I called you."

He asked if Anna Lucia knew what the woman was wearing. She didn't exactly, but let him know about the duffel bag and her complexion.

"It's a good thing you called," the policeman said. "He's pretty bad off. We've got West Penn en route. In the meantime I'd like to ask you a few questions, if that's all right."

"Of course," she said. "Please, come in."

There was no need to tell him everything. He'd seen it too many times. They were drunk and fighting and the girl stabbed him in the chest with a kitchen knife.

Anna Lucia cried, both then and after he'd left. She prayed. God knew that had never been her intent. Maybe it was inevitable, with the two of them. Still, it seemed awful, and needless. The girl would sink back into the underworld of the undocumented. Eddie would live, but would need round-the-clock care; he'd be moved into an assisted-living place in Wilkinsburg, where Anna Lucia would visit him once a month, bringing her famous lasagne.

Once he was gone, she had the rugs torn up and the walls painted a sunny custard yellow. She hired a crew of teenagers from St. Joe's to help her move. She had a lot of stuff, and some of it was heavy: the loveseat with the brocade slipcover, her mother's hutch, the marble-top table. Miraculously, it all fit. She stood in the middle of her new living room, directing the boys—a little more this way, a little more—until she had everything just the way she wanted it.

PART II

Three Rivers

PRAY FOR RAIN

by Nancy Martin
Highland Park

When the floodwaters rose, I went to the grocery store because that's what normal people do. They buy milk and bread and toilet paper, and good girls even buy necessities for their neighbors too.

When I got back from the store around ten in the morning, I parked in the marina lot and grabbed the bag of groceries off the passenger seat. I bailed out into a driving rain and ran across the lot, hoping I looked like a regular person—someone with nothing on her mind but getting through the storm. Before I reached the gate to the boat launch, I wondered how much the flood had washed away.

Over the weekend, a monster hurricane had gathered speed over the gulf and tore a path of waste and death across Louisiana before heading up the Mississippi. The storm's momentum carried heavy weather as far as the Ohio River Valley and finally stalled here in Pittsburgh, where a deluge that smelled like the ocean fell for three days straight. The three rivers rose until the weathermen on television starting yelping about the flood of 1936, sending the whole city's population crowding into the grocery stores to grab supplies.

My old sneakers skidded at the top of the boat launch, and I grabbed the open gate to regain my balance. My houseboat was still there, riding with her lines pulled tight against the cleats of the dock, but the water had come another foot up the concrete launch during the hour it had taken me to get to the store and back. Now the Allegheny swept masses of junk and debris past the few remaining boats tied up at the marina. An empty doghouse floated by, trailing a length of chain. Half a plastic Santa bobbed by on the turmoil of cold brown water. He rolled with the current until one mittened hand rose in the air as if hailing a rescue boat.

"Oh God." I stared at the torrent of garbage rushing on the flood.

From upriver, an enormous tree suddenly roiled up from the surge—muddy roots, thick trunk, branches and all—heading straight for the marina. I caught a breath as the tree slammed into *The Hines*, the old wooden cruiser in the first slip. The shudder reverberated down the whole dock, and unmanned, *The Hines* tore loose from her mooring. The boat spun out into the channel. A jagged hole had been ripped in her hull, and ugly brown water poured through it, rolling the boat lower.

Her owners had fled with nearly everyone else and weren't here to see their grand old lady list down into the river. The swift current swept her past the old salvage yard and the closed steel mill toward the dam. As I watched, the boat struck the dam and split apart. Her glorious upper deck washed over the spillway and disappeared, but the rest of her—the ugly inner workings of the old boat—hung there on the lip, surging and groaning with the flood. Eventually, she'd sink down into the dark water to join the industrial waste that lay at the bottom of this stretch of river. Down there was an underwater junkyard full of horrors I didn't want to think about.

The tree remained by the marina, though, snagged beneath the surface of the floodwaters alongside my boat. The unseen impediment had hooked it like an anchor that shifted only slightly with the rhythm of rising water.

I ran down the concrete steps to the dock. Secured a few slips down from where *The Hines* had been tied, my family's boat rode high on the flood. She wasn't agile on the water or remotely as beautiful as *The Hines*, but we used her to putter downriver to the stadium to wait for fly balls on warm summer nights, so she was still seaworthy. Tied to this dock, I thought she'd be safe.

I thought we'd both be safe.

I grabbed the rail of the boat and leaped across to the deck. I could feel the surge of the flood beneath my unsteady feet. Carefully, I gripped the wet handrail and scrambled around the stern to peer over the opposite rail. The tree lurched in the current there, just a few yards away.

Next door, Ralph Potter came to the shelter of his cabin doorway. He was barefoot and shirtless despite the cold, wearing jeans that rode low on his hips. He grinned and bellowed across the rain. "It's Bible time, Laurie. We're the last ones left! Better pack your stuff and find a hotel room."

I shouted back. "You leaving, Ralphie?"

He laughed and shook his head. He lifted his coffee cup to me—probably holding his morning hair of the dog. "I'll go down with my ship!"

Big talk, but that was Ralphie. He'd come home from Baghdad with a crazy look in his eyes. I knew he sold a little dope to keep body and soul together, but otherwise he hung around the marina drinking, fishing, and sometimes howling at the moon.

I shouted, "What about this tree? It could wipe us all out!"

"Pray for more rain," he called with a cackling laugh. "The only way that tree is leaving is on more water!"

"We're all going to drown!"

More laughing. "Aw, you know more boaters drown from beer than floods!"

He was right, of course. The bodies of most drowned boaters were found with their flies down.

"Did you sleep last night?"

"Slept like a baby! Never heard the thunder or lightning. You?"

No, I hadn't slept much.

The rest of our small community of marina dwellers had wisely hauled their boats out of the water before the river officially hit flood stage and the heaviest debris began to boil past. Yesterday, the fire department had come by to deliver their warnings—get out now, they'd said, because we're not coming back to rescue you later. All of the other regulars obeyed and cleared out before nightfall, except crazy Ralphie. And me.

"If you get scared, you know where you can cuddle up, right?"

I mustered a grin and nodded. "You have groceries?"

"Could use some coffee."

I tossed him a can. He caught it one-handed and cradled it against his bare chest.

Above us, a black pickup truck pulled into the marina and slid to a stop on the slick asphalt. A man in overalls and a parka climbed out of the truck, a cell phone to his ear. He ended the call, then jogged across the parking lot. He pushed through the gate left unlocked by the last hastily fleeing boater.

He shouted my name and peeled back the hood of his coat. It was Nolan McKillip.

Ralphie gave me a raised eyebrow and disappeared into his own boat.

"Now what?" I muttered to myself. But I raised a hand and waved at Nolan.

He bypassed the concrete boat launch where foam and debris surged up the ramp and made for slippery footing. Instead, he rattled down the steps and strode purposefully up the boardwalk, wind at his back. Then he saw the huge tree, riding the water perilously close to my boat.

"Are you crazy?" he shouted over the roar of river. "You're going to get swept away!"

"It's an adventure!" I called, managing a little cheer. "Help me with the lines?"

"What can I do?"

"I'll toss this one to you. Take it up to those pines and tie me off?"

He nodded and held up his hands to receive the line.

I tossed my grocery bag, minus my coffee, into the cabin, then tied a buoy to a length of nylon rope, coiled it up, and threw it expertly—like riding a bike, a skill never forgotten. Nolan, not a boater, caught it clumsily, then struggled up the muddy bank and wrapped the line around a listing pine. He made a hash of the knot, but it would hold. I repeated the process, and he tied off the second line to a different tree.

He came back down the bank, rubbing the crud off his hands, and there was nothing to do but invite him to stay.

"You want to come aboard?" I called, but I heard my own lack of cordiality.

If he heard it too, he ignored it. Nolan jumped from wet dock to thrusting deck, and I made a grab for his arm, but he didn't need steadying. He landed lightly and gathered me up in a hug—quite an experience since he'd taken to pounding iron and feeding a forge in his studio. He had muscle now, and shoulders that felt wonderful to cling to. Folded into his warm frame, I felt safe for an instant.

But then he got a closer look at me, and his eyes widened. "Jesus, what happened?"

"It's nothing. I was trying to start the pump, but the lever kicked back on me." I started to turn away. "A silly mistake. It looks worse than it feels."

Nolan cradled my cheek in his warm hand. "Sweetheart."

I jerked my head to avoid his touch. To take the sting from that little rejection, I smiled up at him and hoped it didn't look false. "Come inside before you get soaked."

In the cabin, I kept my slicker on. "It's not much, but it's home."

He unzipped his parka, shook the rain from his hair, and glanced around. I tried not to imagine what he thought. The cabin looked like the studio apartment of a careless grad student. Or maybe a fugitive on the run. Unmade bed in an alcove and a cluttered kitchen with little more than a hot plate, dorm fridge, microwave, and dishes in the sink. The gray morning light did little to warm the cabin.

It was all a far cry from the converted carriage house where I lived before it all started. On my parents' estate, I'd had the run of the grounds and half the carriage house for a studio. My apartment—furnished with Mother's priceless castoffs and paintings by friends and family—overlooked the swimming pool. At night, with the tiny white lights glittering in the trees, it had been an elegant setting for parties when I felt like having friends over for drinks and talk.

How far away that seemed now, even though the estate was only a mile or two from the houseboat.

Nolan looked toward my easel and paint boxes that were stashed, unused, in a corner with a tangle of buoys and bumpers. A couple of crushed beer cans in the mess finished the picture.

With a frown on his brow, he turned on me. "Laurie, you can't be serious about staying here."

I said, "I know what I'm doing. I've boated all my life."

"But what's the point of staying? This flood is dangerous."

"It's where I live now. It's my home."

"But— Look, your mother called me. She's scared to death."

"She called you, of all people? Why?"

"She worried, that's why. I am too. Staying here—it's nuts."

"I'm not stupid. I'll leave if it gets too bad. Coffee?"

"It's not just the flood," Nolan said. "She said Dennis called the house."

I snatched up my grocery bag and pushed aside some dishes to make room for it on the kitchen counter. Then I fumbled with the coffee pot, trying to tamp down panic.

"She said Dennis was drunk on the phone with her. Has he been here?"

"What fool would come down here in weather like this?" I mustered some humor and gave him a shaky smile over my shoulder.

Nolan still frowned. "We're afraid for your safety."

"So am I," I said lightly. "Which is why I went to the police. Do you mind if I zap some coffee instead of making fresh?"

"I don't care. Laurie—"

"Look, I appreciate your concern. I really do. But I'm not helpless. Why does everybody treat me as if I am? The police will take care of Dennis. We have to let the legal system work."

Nolan caught my arm and pulled me around. "Forget about coffee. Talk to me."

Looking up into his worried face, I tried to recall how

long I'd known Nolan. He'd been in my orbit since before I could remember—the son of family friends in a rarified social circle. When my grandfather died the year I was sixteen, he'd come solemnly to the funeral with his father—both in suits and ties—and we'd eyed each other with covert interest. Months later, he smuggled me a drink from the bar at a cousin's wedding at a swanky country club. When he gave me the glass, Nolan noticed the paint under my nails, and we'd gone outside to talk about art in the evening air while the music played.

His older brothers went into business and law, but Nolan had grown up artistic and intuitive. With a discerning eye and passion too. Playing rugby evolved into building gigantic steel mobiles—the kind corporations bought to display in their impressive headquarters. He and I had gone our separate ways, but there had been potential between us. For a while.

Nolan watched me, his expression going very still. "Tell me the truth. Did Dennis come here to see you?"

"Heavens, no."

Whether he believed me or not, I couldn't be sure. He released my arm and said, "Your mother says there's a gun on the boat. Is that true?"

"I have no idea. There might have been one years ago, but surely not anymore."

"I have one, if you need it."

That surprised me. But I said, "I wouldn't know how to use a gun."

Nolan's gaze didn't waver. "I made some calls after your mother contacted me. I talked to his brother. Laurie, Dennis phoned from this location last night."

Suddenly I couldn't breathe. "How do you know that?"

"He has a fancy app on his cell phone—a GPS. So does his

brother. He made the call, Laurie. Did you see him?"

"Of course not."

"But the call."

"He might have come around the marina." Uncertainly, I glanced out the window and tried to remember. How long had I left the curtains open last night? I gathered my wits and said, "Nolan, I don't want you mixed up in this."

"In what?"

"Dennis and me."

"Jesus, are you back together with him?"

"God, no."

"Then why—?"

"Please, I don't want you to—Dennis will go away eventually, but until then, you need to keep your distance."

Nolan seized me by the elbows, his hands insistent. "I can help, Laurie. I'll break his neck if he hurts you again."

I smiled. For all his size, I couldn't see Nolan hurting anyone. He was too sweet. Sometimes so sweet my teeth ached.

But Dennis? He had swept into the city like a pirate from New York and conned a local art dealer into giving him a share in a gallery. Then the hoodwinking started. Nothing could ever be proved, of course, but there were commissions stolen, artists cheated, buyers angry. The gallery owner retired hastily and fled to Florida. Dennis's life-of-the-party personality and undeniable sex appeal—for both men and women, it turned out—kept him riding high a little longer.

He'd come courting me before his real trouble started. The reputation of my family—painters, all of us, especially Daddy, a portraitist and teacher at the university—made me a kind of blue blood in the city creative class, something Dennis needed to keep going. Respectability, that's what I'd brought to the match. And he'd brought—well, something

I had avoided since a stormy love affair fell apart two years ago. Sex, at first. The kind that made me lose my head. And more excitement too—one temptation after another to lure me deeper into his world.

But Dennis soon ran the gallery into the ground and took my good name with it.

The first time he hit me had been at Thanksgiving. His frustration boiled over. Somehow his financial problems were all my fault. He knocked out my eye tooth—humiliating as much as painful.

"Are you in some kind of trouble, Laurie?" Dr. Feingold had asked, there in his dental office. His gentle eyes were worried behind his round-framed glasses.

I lied to him. Told him I'd fallen off a ladder while setting up the Christmas tree.

During the holidays my family intervened—expressing genteel concern and dismay. A restraining order, they urged. So I went to the police station and blushed the whole time I told impassive officers my dirty story. They asked awful questions. About the sex. Had I liked it at first and then got second thoughts? What else? I told them as much as I could stand, and that he'd begun to hit me. The police took photos of my bruises. I admitted that he'd threatened to do worse.

The restraining order didn't stop Dennis, though. I'd called 911 and had him arrested twice—the first time during a Twelfth Night party where friends watched aghast—which only made him more furious with me.

My mother started having angina attacks. What could I do but move off the family estate to spare her? So I'd come to the boat and hoped I could resolve things myself.

In a hard voice, Nolan said, "Did you see him last night, Laurie? You can trust me."

"No."

"Because . . ."

I saw a change in Nolan's face. "What?" I asked. "What's wrong?"

Nolan turned his head away. "He was supposed to meet me last night. To give me something."

"Give you what?"

After a heartbeat, Nolan said, "He had pictures."

"From the gallery?"

"No."

It didn't take much to figure out what he meant. Photos. Blackmail. The word made my insides twist with pain. I'd brought ugliness into so many lives. First Dennis had gone to my family and now to Nolan, threatening to show my mother what I'd become. All this awfulness because I'd yearned to walk on the wild side.

I said, "He wanted you to pay him for pictures."

"Yes."

"Of me."

"Yes."

I knew exactly which photographs he meant. A night long ago, when Dennis was still deliciously naughty and fun, he'd snapped a few shots in bed. After I'd had too much wine. When it hadn't taken a lot of convincing. Dennis brought out something in me that I then realized had been lurking inside all along.

My face burning, I said, "Did he show them to you?"

"Only one." Nolan's voice sounded hollow.

"Well, I hope it was a good one."

I shoved through the door, and slammed it back on its hinges. On the deck, I gulped fresh air to fight down nausea. The water was rougher than before, but the rain had let up a little. I grabbed the railing for support. The tree had rolled away from the boat, I thought. Maybe the thing that snagged it had shifted too. I fought down the nausea that rushed up from inside me

Nolan came out of the cabin and said nothing.

He'd never think of me the same way again, that was for sure. I'd never be the pretty girl at the country club, sipping cocktails on the veranda and talking about the Impressionists. Him brushing a ladybug from my yellow dress, thinking I was the kind of girl he could take home to his family.

In a while, I said, "How much were you going to pay him?"

"It doesn't matter."

"That kind of thing never stops, you know. You pay him once, he'll come back for more until you're broke."

Gently, Nolan put his hand on the small of my back. His touch felt as if he wanted to go dancing. "Let me take you to your mother's house, just for a couple of nights, okay? When the weather settles down, we can—"

"No," I said.

"I want to help."

"I don't need help!"

"The hell you don't."

"Not from you," I snapped and spun around.

He pulled his hand away and tightened it into a fist. "You're not the only one who has a dark side, Laurie. Maybe I'm not who you think I am either."

If only he were, my problems might be over.

Ralphie came back outside of his own houseboat across the dock from mine. He'd put on a shirt and shoes, but that didn't make him look any more respectable than before. His ball cap was on backwards, with greasy hair sticking out around the back of his neck. He made a big show of stretching his arm over his head and yawning. His jeans rode low, showing a line of pubic hair on his belly.

Then he called, "Everything okay over there, Laurie?"

"Who's he?" Nolan asked me.

"We're fine, Ralphie!"

Ralphie squinted at us. "Your friend bothering you?"

"He was just leaving."

"Laurie—"

"Go, Nolan," I said, low-voiced. "I didn't ask you to come. I don't want you here. I don't want you mixed up in my problems."

"Too late," Nolan replied. But he turned away. He pulled his car keys from a pocket. "Will you call me if you have to get away fast? I can be down here in half an hour. I'll pick you up, take you home."

I'm never going home, I almost said aloud. It would be like dragging barrels of poison through the front door.

But I said, "Thank you."

"Is your cell phone charged?"

"Go, Nolan. I'll be fine."

He went. He glanced back over his shoulder once, doubtfully taking in Ralphie again. For all I knew, he wondered if I'd given up Dennis, and rejected him too, for the likes of Ralphie now, a houseboat rat who drank too much. Who dealt drugs, peed in the river when the need arose, who ate Slim Jims for dinner and probably never heard of the Impressionists.

When Nolan had climbed into his truck, started the engine, and backed out of his parking space, Ralphie vaulted over the railing of his own boat and landed on the dock in his sneakers. His sweatshirt read, *Steelers*, in faded black and yellow letters.

He said, "Old boyfriend?"

"I guess that's what you could call him."

"Not anymore, you mean?"

"Not anymore."

"You have a lot of those, don't you?"

Ralphie had a whippy kind of strength in his body and a loose, happy smile. He might have been a sexy ladykiller once, before he went to seed. He leaned playfully on my railing, absorbing the surge of the boat with his arms. But his gaze was full of something darker than mischief.

When I didn't answer, he said, "Water's still rising."

"I see that."

"I expect it'll come up a few more feet before it's all over."

"Yes."

"If we get more rain, and then it'll wash everything away. Maybe us too, but everything else, for sure."

He nodded at the tree, still riding the river's current alongside the dock. The branches twisted, the few remaining leaves wriggling as if in death throes.

Around the tree, the water ran muddy brown, full of silt from upstream, so it was impossible to see below the surface of the river.

But eventually the water would clear, and the view to the bottom would be unobstructed. Dennis's car would be clearly visible.

Last night, when the car disappeared into the dark water at the end of the boat launch, I thought it was gone for good. But choking back tears, I had watched the turn signal flash for hours. At some point the light stopped blinking like a heartbeat—short-circuited at last. Or maybe the car had rolled over, burying the light in mud. Whichever it was, I had finally gone to bed.

But this morning I had seen ripples on the surface of the river where the car lay submerged.

When the tree had slammed into the sunken car I thought maybe, just maybe, the tree might push the car out into the channel, deeper into the river where it would never be seen or found. If the river's current strengthened, if the tree continued to push, perhaps the car would wash into oblivion.

If it didn't wash away, the car would be discovered when the flood receded and everybody came back to put their boats into the river again.

I was in trouble. Deep.

Ralphie said, "We just need another day of rain. Then it'll wash his car away. Nobody'll ever see it."

He grinned at me, and I felt my heart lurch.

Conversationally, he asked, "Did you shoot him first?"

"Yes." I swallowed hard.

Ralphie shrugged. "I was drunk last night, and maybe I slept like a rock, but something woke me up. Must have been your gun. I came outside and watched. I saw everything. You dragging him up to his car, shoving him behind the wheel, putting the transmission in neutral. Where's the gun now?"

"In—in the car."

Ralphie slipped a wet lock of my hair behind my ear, and his touch lingered there. "Was he dead when you pushed the car down the ramp?"

"I'm not sure."

If Dennis had lived long enough to make a phone call from the sinking car—perhaps desperately dialing as the cold water enveloped his bleeding body—well, I couldn't think about that.

The river surged around us with a dull yet rhythmic roar. Listening to it, I decided it sounded like the pulse of God.

Ralphie took off his ball cap and plunked it on my head. He was smiling at me. "Don't worry, honey. If this rain keeps up, the car will wash down to the dam and get lost in all the crap down there. Nobody'll ever find it. Or him."

He put his arm around me, nuzzled my throat, and breathed the fumes of his first beer of the day into my ear. He ignored my shudder.

"Let's go inside for a while, huh?" Ralphie slid his hand down inside the back of my jeans and cupped my butt. "You'd like that, right? We'll fool around a little, you and me. Get to know each other better. And all we have to do is pray it keeps raining, right?"

"Right," I said.

A MINOR EXTINCTION

BY PAUL LEE

Carrick

The river that persisted namelessly in his dreams seemed to be all rivers at once, black and collusive and oceanic. It carried him along a swift path beneath a star-spattered firmament, and though he knew the water to be ice cold it seemed to his skin to have been stripped of temperature. He was a silhouette projected on the water, in conveyance to a place that was strange and logical, cruel and intimate. And how the stars teemed so impassively above him as he lay in bed, drowning in sleep . . . how they burned small and cold and bright in all of that unfathomable blackness, like grains of fossilized fire strewn in pitch, as the river pulled him across the earth in a fugue of stark and limitless dread and longing.

He was working in a room of increasing white when he was told the latest news about the elder Gorski brother. It was noon, and they were painting another empty old house in Carrick whose inhabitant had moved or died. The floors were sheathed in plastic. The interior walls had sallowed to the shade of animal fat, and, hearing the news, Mark continued to work as though he had not heard a thing, rewetting the long-handled roller in the pan and applying to the stale walls lucent strips of dripping, viscous white, a slathered rendering of reversed time. "Couldn't stop his brain swelling," the other painter was saying sidelong from his perch on the stepladder.

He seemed unslighted by Mark's silence, even a little defer-
ent to it; he had also gone to Carrick High years ago and was
still held by the residual sway of Mark's single year of seniority
and former status as a varsity hockey player—the old teenage
hierarchy. "Real sad about that family," he was saying.

A rumor had been circulating that Zacharias Gorski had
been, uncharacteristically, blind drunk while driving home
through Mount Oliver three nights ago. Mark had heard only
that he had hit a tree and been thrown from his car, but the
rest seemed as clear to him as if he had been in the passenger seat: the upstanding surviving brother, college-educated
and betrothed, swept down a fast black road almost against
volition, headlights swinging wildly around a sharp corner,
propelled into the night by drunkenness and the brute laws
of random chance. It was as if Mark was witness to the still-
conscious Zacharias being launched headlong through ex-
ploding glass and flung into the hollow that the headlights
had dug out of the darkness, as if he heard Zacharias's skull
striking something hard, a rock or a tree trunk, at the edge of
those woods. He heard it as the same sound—not an identical
sound but the very same sound repeated—as the one he had
heard when the younger brother died, when Mark accidentally
killed Levi Gorski eight years ago. It was as though the eight
years were a canyon and he was just now hearing the echo of
the original impact undiminished from the opposite side. *Sad
about that family.* And from here he could see that irrevocable
night occurring across the canyon. Seventeen-year-old Levi
shivering skinny and half-naked by the river, his face lit up
by the flashlight, downy black mustache soaked in mud and
bloodied snot. And underneath those vast stars made tiny by
distance, beside the strand of water that was the Monongahela: just the slightest flick of movement. The shear streak

of the Maglite, a small figure toppling backward, fragile head meeting the edge of a rock somewhere in the dark. And if that rock had not been there. *Or if I had not been here.*

If Mark Braun had not been here he would be a twenty-six-year-old Korean living amid a countryful of Koreans, maybe attending electrical school the way he had been planning for years now, and perhaps knowing of Pittsburgh only by way of Hines Ward. Levi Gorski would still be living, probably still a fuck-up, and Zacharias Gorski would not be brain-dead. But instead Mark was adopted by an American couple before he learned to speak and transported from Korea to Pittsburgh, brought here to be the Chinese boy in Carrick with the German last name. And instead he was raised on fish sticks and pierogies, surviving all the bullying and taunting, learning eventually to mock the few other Asian kids he encountered with even greater cruelty. And instead he grew up athletic and crew-cut and thick-necked and played hockey, never a star player but always solid enough to stay off the bench. He guzzled beer and bum wine with the best of them. Yet on some level he still sensed, even in people he had known since childhood, that they continued to perceive in him a touch of the simulated life—that, to them, each perfectly formed American word that came from his mouth remained perennially a small astonishment, the uncanny product of some tortuous craftsmanship that was occurring somewhere behind that face.

And there was something of the weight of this continental displacement behind the blow that killed Levi Gorski—Levi, a mangy kid who was rumored to have once eaten a sporkful of shit for twenty bucks, who had obliquely called Mark's then-girlfriend Abigail—a white girl—a "gook" after she whirled and called him shiteater for squeezing himself indecently past her in the hall. Mark had betrayed nothing as she recounted the incident to him later that night. Outwardly he had only mirrored her casual disgust. But already he had felt himself being taken up by a fast-moving current, one he mistook for self-determined rage, a current which seemed to carry him to—and then leave him just a few beats after—the moment that found him by the river, flanked by two of his hockey buddies, drunk on Mad Dog 20/20 with the Maglite poised above Levi's head. They had earlier found Levi smoking by himself in the dark near his house, the three boys crudely flush with purpose and wildness after four-wheeling through Mount Oliver in Nathaniel's truck. It was still an incipient spring, a night when the wind seemed to be cutting in from the expired winter. They had forced Levi into the backseat like mobsters and sped to Riverfront Park, bloodying his nose along the way, with Isaac nearly singing about how they would beat him unconscious and leave him by the river to freeze. But Mark later understood that he was impelled toward the scene of Levi's death not by the exuberance of adolescent violence but by the force of that ruthless current, which proved strong enough to sweep up the other three boys along with him, strong enough even to deliver Levi's older brother to his fate eight years later.

They had parked near the Birmingham Bridge on a bleak vacant street lined with warehouses. In warmer weather they might have seen another parked car or two, signs of teenagers tucked away in the dark to smoke weed or make out, but on this night they were alone. They forced Levi to the riverside, their victim first squirming and yelling, but after being smacked quiet letting his boots drag in what seemed a parody of nonviolent resistance, then finally stumbling along with his head bowed: the consciously bland submission of someone, outnumbered and outpowered, who can at last only hope that his aggressors will soon grow bored of his meekness. The river, opening up wide before them, ran calm and tranquil, its edges lapping up in ragged doglike waves onto the dirt, and with the Maglite switched on they turned and navigated the black thread of scraggly wilderness along the water while shoving Levi shirtless into the jagger bushes, the bugs biting, behind them the civilized world quietly receding, seemingly from existence, the four of them hiking through that wooded darkness until about ten minutes later they stopped randomly at some sufficiently removed spot that afterward seemed predestined, and Mark, before even willing it, swung hard at Levi and knocked him to the hard-packed dirt, maybe even as surprised as he by the connecting impact of that first real uninhibited effort to inflict human damage. There had hung a beat of silence when he hit the ground. Then the three lit upon him, kicking and thrashing at the prostrate shape in the dark. The memory of this remained for Mark only as shredded sensation: the scribble of the flashlight over Levi's curled backside, the panting of exertion, the guttural grunting when they would wedge a hard kick in the soft of his belly. They forced his head up and shoved a fistful of riversludge into his mouth, calling him shiteater, then batted him around again, all of them reluctant to be the first one to let up. And strangely, Mark could not even remember now whether or not he had felt any rage over Levi's offense while in the act of assaulting him, any remnant of that burst of raw heat that had originally resolved him to beat this white boy into repentance. It was as though the record of that retributive heat, if there had indeed been any, had been expunged by the running river, leaving for memory only a cold, passionless violence even more savage for its bloodlessness. As though passion in the end had no bearing upon the governing forces of life and death, and at the river the four had unknowingly given themselves up in violent ritual to that greater logic which was inexorable in its progression. And it was on this force that Mark pulled Levi to his feet for the last time—his motility gone sluggish and boozy, his shivering torso thorn-scratched and slick from sweat and mud, the four of them in that instant a tableau of miniature figures seen from across a canyon of eight years—and without thinking brought the butt of the Maglite down on his head. Levi fell—seemed to backfall a distance far deeper than his standing height, with a force far heavier than his falling weight. They heard a blunter, meatier echo of the blow that sent him down, then nothing.

We killed him

Mark you fucking killed him

Instantly the current that had brought him here seemed to desert him, to drain away in a final roar and expose an underlying quiet that he had not known he had not been hearing, the ever-present quiet of the dirt and the stars and their bodies quietly alive. A barge lowed somewhere on the water. They swung the body blindly into the river and left, scared as hell, and no one saw them. Afterward no one suspected them. It was only later that Mark began to gain a crude understanding that the current had not left him at all; it had only merged into a larger course, one in which he was no longer an active mechanism but a thing powerlessly adrift, too small and too integrated to perceive what engulfed him as anything separate from the carriage of existence itself.

He was driving the company truck toward the South Side after work, last week's snow still shrinking on the edges of the road. The heater was rasping. It was an old pickup of an indeterminate grade of black, a rattling, smoking steel thing with a busted radio and cracked vinyl seats and faded lettering on the sides. The windshield was cold and sunbrushed with the last of the slanting daylight. Normally he took the bus home, but today he had volunteered to close the shop, then taken the truck out when the others had gone, with hardly a thought given to consequence or purpose.

He drove now with the half-formed notion of going to a bar, but was thinking of Levi's murder and seeing everything around him, the entire world as he knew it, as what the murder had left behind in its wake. One of his science teachers, who had liked to tell Mark that he could go far in life if he only applied himself, had once said that the course of the universe was like a cosmic game of billiards. And Mark was thinking of this now, of pool balls ricocheting again and again in endlessly multiplying accident. Thinking, *He's dead Mark you killed him*. Thinking of Abigail, how they had broken up soon after, how she had then ricocheted until she had become engaged to Zacharias, how Mark had thought her ricocheting had stopped then. Thinking how the ricocheting had now killed Zacharias too, and knowing now that its reverberation would never cease—that it would one day become unattributable to the murder, but only because it would exceed the limits of human calculation and memory.

As he neared the East Carson bars, he found himself turning onto the narrow street on which stood UPMC South Side, where Zacharias was lying somewhere, brain-dead. He found a vacant spot by the curb and, from the idling truck, gazed up at the building's turreted façade without intention, only thinking in a mild stupor that this was where the Gorski family would finally be blotted out. He was recalling the classic illustration of human evolution, the monkey uncrouching by increments toward the apotheosis that was man, and in his mind he pictured the Gorskis' ancestral line in the same way: the descendents springing up one after another through dark millennia in an unbroken and resolute linear procession, only to be suddenly extinguished by the repercussive force of his own trivial and incredulous hand. Permanently annihilated. There would be whole branches of people who would now never come into being, whom the world would never even know to miss. The idea was almost unfathomable to him in its simple desolation.

When a few minutes had passed, he twisted off the engine and sat in the violently ensuing silence, sensing the tiny clustering of the oncoming dusk, the near-imperceptible way it began its purple bloodying of the air. He continued to stare up at the hospital, as if by staring enough he might see Zacharias. At any moment he expected to restart the engine and drive to the bar, but his expectation was devoid of will, as though the decision to leave would be made by someone other than himself.

When she came out, he did not immediately recognize her. She was just another figure emerging from the building, small in her puff of a white jacket, like something blown out onto the sidewalk. There was an air of relief about her, something he had noticed in others who had exited, some registering of freedom, but in her it somehow seemed intentioned, the exhalation exaggerated for her own witnessing, as if by feigning it, the actual relief, and then the actual freedom, would follow. He tracked her absently as she walked in his direction, but it was only when she stepped in front of the truck to cross the street that he recognized her as Abigail. He watched a few moments longer, unmoving and unthinking, before abruptly quitting the truck and walking after her.

She was proceeding hurriedly, cutting toward the next

block through the small sitting area opposite the hospital, and he followed as if pulled by the slipstream, not calling out, not knowing what he would say when he caught up to her. They had not remained close after they broke up those years ago. Their affair, which had lasted maybe seven months, had seemed a thing of real substance by high school standards, the first convincing romance for both, and perhaps would have continued had it not been for the murder. He remembered it as a sustained flash of heat against the cold, beginning in the waning warmth of late late summer and fizzling in the spring, in full bloom only in fall and winter. It had seemed to have its own unspoken logic, by which their fierce rifts were graced with the same intimacy as their tenderest moments. Their arguments in the halls had reached levels of violence that bordered on parody, taking on the air of staged teen dramas in which they were secretly witting actors; on campus they became as famous for their public fights as for their public affection. Their theatricality—the cheek both burning from a slap and imprinted with lipstick—had made itself the trademark of their relationship, seemed crucial to its continuing survival, and this may have set the precedent for Mark's brutal response to Levi's offense, because between them there had never been any room for the middle ground.

They had broken up soon after. As he followed her now he was thinking of how they had never spoken over the years, seeming almost to realize it for the first time. She had become a neighborhood fixture to him, someone he saw with inevitable regularity around Carrick and East Carson, and in the process she had entered that strange realm of once-familiar things that have fallen into conspicuous obscurity. He had heard through friends about her father's brain cancer—a bad headache one morning, buried five months later—and her engagement to Zacharias, but had otherwise rarely thought about her directly, instead remembering Abigail and that segment of his past as a single crude impression of vivid color and heat. He followed her for another short block, muted by the years. There were stretches of the sidewalk still crusted over with ice, but she moved quickly, incautiously. At the corner she crossed the street to the first available bar, a dingy corner dive with a white shingled overhang, and pushed through its palm-smudged door.

He stopped, lingering on the opposite side, but in a minute Abigail reappeared, clutching a weighted paper bag with both hands. She saw him standing across the street then and quickly looked away as if she hadn't, as had been their custom. But now he held his gaze, unmoving as she crossed back to his side, the beer bottles clinking in her bag, and finally she looked back at him when it could no longer be avoided, her expression hard but unable to fully conceal her incredulousness. "Mark," she said ironically. He had not looked at her this closely in eight years, but he felt no tug of old emotion, only a defamiliarized recollection of intimacy. While most people he knew, including himself, had gained some heft around the jaw since high school, Abigail had grown bonier, shedding the shapeless skinniness of her youth for a thinness that seemed lighter and frailer and more severe, giving an impression of bones growing hollow. She was not wearing makeup today, and her face had that raw scrubbed appearance of women who are rarely seen without it.

"I heard," he said. "About Zacharias."

She studied him for a moment without speaking. He had not been friends with Zacharias, who was two years older and had been away at college at IUP when Levi died. Nor had Mark decided upon an explanation for his sudden appearance on this empty corner, still in his work clothes, his pants and boots splotched with dry paint. But she showed no intention of asking, instead seemed to be trying to deduce it from his face. Her tone was even and empty of sarcasm when she responded: "So you know I'm engaged to a vegetable then."

He shifted uncertainly. "I was thinking maybe I could see him," he said then without thinking, unsure whether he asked because he could think of nothing else to say or because this was the reason he had come.

She gave him a strange look. "You wanna see Zach?" But then the look passed from her face, as though she had decided that her wondering was not worth the effort. She looked back at the hospital. "Well I'm having one of these over there first. Then if you still want, I'll take you up to see him."

He carried the bag for her as they returned. The outdoor sitting area was empty. She chose one of the maroon benches farthest from the street, then pulled two bottles of Yuengling from the bag and handed one to Mark. They sat and drank from the green bottles as the light began its slow fade, their breaths steaming and cooling in the air. For a while neither spoke, just sat looking at the hospital entrance as Abigail peeled the labels from her bottle and flicked the pieces onto the ground. The silence gathered between them in stealthy accumulation, first incurring a palpable weight, then growing fat with character, until it seemed to ape the chronic silence that had broken their romance years ago, to echo the abrupt silence that had announced Levi's death by the river, to imagine the unknowable silence that now whirled in Zacharias's head, until at last the silence grew too heavy to continue, seemed to collapse upon itself, and Mark spoke reflexively as though responding to physical law.

"I remember when I went to his brother's funeral and

Zacharias went up to the coffin." He was not looking at her, but he continued to speak. "Up till that point he was rock-solid—you know. The big brother back from college, shaking hands with everyone and taking charge. But when it was his turn to go up to the coffin and look at Levi's picture, it was like the whole thing just crumbled. He was just standing in front of it for a second or two, but then his hands went up to his face, he almost slapped himself, and suddenly he was all hunched over and shaking. And we were all just sitting there watching him. And after a while his dad had to take him away, and we never saw him again."

She said nothing for a few moments, letting his words grow strange in the air. "Well," she said finally, "I don't know why you ever went to that funeral anyway."

Mark hesitated, took a slug of beer.

Then her tone softened. "Let's not start this, this kind of talk, the dead mourning the dead. Not yet."

"All right."

"I mean, you didn't even know him," she said, her voice stirring again. "Or Levi, really. God, I haven't even seen you for years."

"What do you mean?" He looked at her now. "I see you around all the time."

"Maybe you saw someone else," she said, not meeting his eyes.

"You saying you didn't notice the Chinese guy hanging around Carrick?"

She let out a familiar sigh. "I'm not saying anything, Mark." She finished her beer and stood up, and in the fading light he recognized some agitated kink in her stance that for an instant seemed to telescope the past eight years into something graspable. "You still want to see him or not?" she asked. He downed the last of his beer and followed her inside, leaving their bottles sitting empty on the bench.

When they reached the room that contained Zacharias, Abigail took the paper bag from Mark and set it down in the hallway by the edge of the open door. Then she motioned him in. He entered to find Zacharias's parents and grandfather seated in a row of three chairs along the wall by the bed, on which Zacharias lay as if asleep. They looked up at him when he came in, the grandfather's expression one of foggy incomprehension, something distantly savage in his decrepitude, and the parents reflexively smiling the feeble and exhausted smile that they had been practicing together for days, perhaps mistaking him for one of the hospital staff. They looked small and supplicant in their chairs beside Zacharias, whose substantial figure was stretched across the bed, seeming the size of the three of them combined. Abigail appeared behind Mark but lingered in the doorframe, saying, "This is one of Zach's friends." The parents nodded feebly at him, still smiling and saying nothing.

Mark stepped toward the bed. He had been this close to Zacharias only a few times, and only by accident, brushing past him in the halls between classes, or later vying with him for the attention of a bartender at Mario's. His head was almost comically bandaged, the gauze baring what seemed a niggardly amount of face, from the eyelids to just below the lower lip. But even on this meager stretch of skin the shattered windshield and fatal trauma were fully manifest: his face was like a random side of a bruised pear, finely lacerated and discolored, softly misshapen, his closed eyes swollen and seeming sealed over with wax. A pair of tubes ran from the machine to converge in his mouth, force-feeding vital gases.

"Who is that?" the grandfather roared suddenly to no one,

his jaundiced eyes seizing upon Mark in what appeared a kind of vague terror. The mother patted his hand and murmured, "A friend of Zach's." The grandfather grunted.

Mark glanced back at Abigail, who was leaning against the doorframe. She was not looking at him or anything else in the room. Instead her gaze was fixed on some faraway point beyond the walls, and her foot was steadily tapping the floor, betraying impatience. But framed within the doorway she appeared almost serene, and would have been a portrait of female serenity had she been painted in this moment, with her tapping foot stilled by the fixed colors. When she met his eyes her face grew rigid, breaking the illusion. She shot him a look demanding they leave.

He looked down again at Zacharias, taking in once more all of that mortal irreparability, seeing him now—a dead lump of living tissue—as the blunt implement of the Gorskis' final erasure. Then Mark stepped away. The grandfather peered at him as if seeing him for the first time, blurting again, "Who is that?"—the dusty, fading patriarch, registering in perhaps only an intermittent glimmer the totality of his posterity's irreversible failure. This time no one answered him. The polite feeble smile reappeared on the parents' faces when they saw that Mark was leaving, and suddenly he felt sickened with some mixture of guilt and pity and scorn and revulsion. It was a shiteating smile, he realized. It was a smile of shiteating surrender, a sick swallowing-and-grinning expression of utter powerlessness, of private, implacable misery. They continued to smile gruesomely, smiling beside their dead son, and Mark retreated after Abigail, muttering some goodbye.

Outside, the night had been consummated. The stars shone cold and clear, almost ringing to Mark with some deep familiarity, some deeply familiar mystery. They went to sit inside the truck to drink the remaining beers, and Mark turned on the ignition to run the heater. The truck stammered intransigently, then fired on with a massive metal roar, then fell into its steady idled shuddering. They sat in the dark, drinking.

Abigail pulled her feet up onto the seat and hugged her knees. "I can't take it anymore, just sitting there staring at him," she said quietly, almost to herself. "It's like we're trying to stare at him till we stop seeing anything there."

"Yeah," said Mark, his mind elsewhere. How impassively the stars had witnessed the murder, those stars that night by the river. And I remember those stars, he was thinking, knowing that they had been clinging to that same black sky for eight years unchanged.

Mark are you fucked in the head you fucking killed him
Throw him in the river we have to
Grab his legs
Hurry

He did not understand the science behind the scrolling map of the sky, but he knew that the stars above the hospital now were not the same ones from that night; he did not recognize them. He was thinking, I remember the stars from that night and they are still there only because I remember them. If I forget them they will cease to exist.

He and Abigail sat in the truck, quieted by uncertainty. He knew that when they finished the six-pack there would be no more reason for them to remain; Abigail would leave the truck to go become a widow, and Mark would drive the truck back to the shop, maybe stop by a bar to get drunk, and to him this seemed incomplete, though he could not have explained what he was waiting for. But he made no move to alter this course, only sitting and thinking quietly, And if I exist in the memory of those stars as they exist in mine, if they can remember me only because I remember them. And if I cease to remember them. Finally thinking, Yes, if I cease to remember them then they will have to cease to remember me. Then it will be as if that night never happened. As if I had not killed him.

And then something was quietly activated in him. Word- lessly he shifted the truck into gear and pulled out into the street in a disembodied decision to simply drive. Abigail did not ask where they were going, consenting with reciprocal wordlessness, and when he turned west onto East Carson she gazed out the window as if she had not seen the strip a thou- sand times before, as if she were new to town, all of that ex- clusive tangled neon slung low on the buildings, brazen and eye-catching and aloof. For a while the pink light permeated the truck with something sentimental, a soft electric intima- tion of lapsed time and lapsed memory. Then it seeped away as they cleared the strip, and the night seemed to reemerge all around them. The road angled northward, and soon they were driving parallel to the Monongahela, and when they drove past the confluence, both gazed out at the Point as they always did here and would continue to do for the rest of their lives: the sight of the whole city, at the will of the rivers, con- verging in a crush of architecture into a single spew of water. And then it passed behind them, the city darkening like a heap of embers dying, and then they were driving along the Ohio River under black sky, the stars fanning, and soon they were separated from the water by only a bare set of railroad tracks.

Abigail spoke, still looking out at the river which ran long and dark beside them. "We were house shopping," she said, just audible over the truck. "Every weekend we'd go out and look at houses. Once we even bid on one."

"Where?" asked Mark when she fell quiet.

"Carrick. Of course Carrick. He was actually more into the whole thing than I was. He didn't want us to get married and then have to come back to the same apartment." Then she added, "He would have been a good father."

Mark nodded, though she was not looking at him to see it. The road continued to grow darker, the stars clearer. He remembered that he had seen her with Zacharias on a weekend afternoon not long ago, conferring in front of a house with some woman in a red pantsuit. He had thought nothing of it then, but felt now as though he had stolen a glimpse into an abrogated future, being for a moment privy to the unstomachable processes of fate permanently altering its course.

"I need to move out of Pittsburgh," she said. "I don't ever want to see those houses again, and they're all over Carrick. I can't keep living here."

As they crossed the creek into McKees Rocks, a smaller road opened up, following the bend of the river. Mark swerved onto it, rattling across the train tracks, then pulled off the road onto the first gravel yard that sat off the riverbank, one still patched with snow and littered with beached rundown motorboats. He stopped the truck and climbed out into the night, his face turned up to the sky as the gravel crunched under his boots. The wind was sweeping raw and hard across the water but he did not feel cold. Five miles downstream from where he had once deposited Levi Gorski into the water, he was staring at the stars now to see whether he would recognize them, thinking, If they are not the same, then when I die my memory will die and their memory of me will die with it. They shone clearer here than ever, each a vivid puncture in the night, but as he looked and strained to look, they seemed to grow only increasingly ambiguous in arrangement, until he found he could no longer see anything in them, could not recognize whether they were familiar or strange, until they seemed just meaningless points of light spread flat and trivial across the sky.

He had left the headlights on. For a while Abigail sat in the fading warmth of the truck, watching his shape moving then going distant in the dark. He seemed submerged in it, a dimly rendered figure sluggish and incipient in dark liquid. From within the truck she could hear the wind battering the windows with an animal energy, wild and invisible. "What are you doing?" she finally called out to him, rolling the window down a crack, but her voice seemed to fly away in the wrong direction.

And standing in the untamed grass that lined the river, Mark thought he saw something floating silently on the water.

You killed him, didn't you? he heard Abigail say out of the darkness, her voice almost inaudible in the wind.

He froze, something terrible expanding in his chest.

Did you kill him? she murmured.

When he turned he saw her climbing out of the truck in the distance and walking toward him against the wind with her hair blowing back, clutching a beer in her hand. For a moment she was lit garishly by the headlights. She stepped from the gravel onto the concrete between them, and then he saw her suddenly going down on a patch of ice, falling messily but somehow retaining an impression of lightness, like a bird knocked to the earth by a gust. When he went back to her she was still sitting on the concrete with her hand held to her stomach. Her mouth was skewed and rigid. "Goddamn ice," she said. She took a stubborn drink from her beer, which she had somehow managed to save, before allowing him to help her up. Her hand remained on her stomach, and her mouth remained rigid.

"You all right?" he said.

She shook her head.

"I can drive you back."

She shook her head again and walked stiffly ahead of him toward the river. He joined her where she stood on the grass gazing at the sparse black trees of Brunot Island. "I'm fucking pregnant," she said finally over the wind. The words seemed to race toward some distant point behind them at a hundred miles an hour. "I hadn't even told him yet," she added. "Haven't told anyone."

The island jutted like some malignant outgrowth from the middle of the river.

"I'm getting rid of it obviously," she said, then took another swallow of beer as if to drive the point home. As the bottle fell back to her side he reached to take it from her, attempting in the last instant to mask the effort in casualness as if they had been sharing the bottle. She let him take it. But when he raised it to his own lips he found it mostly empty, the last mouthful of beer warmed by her hand. She looked at him strangely, then moved away from him, wandering upstream beside the black water, just beyond the reach of its ragged waves.

Something began to take shape dimly at the back of his mind. He turned the empty bottle over in his hands, then pulled his arm back and hurled it by the neck. He could not see it fly, but he thought he could hear it ringing for a few seconds, the whispering friction of air on glass, until it was blotted out by the water. When he glanced over, Abigail was the clearest object in the near distance, her white winter jacket catching the scant trickle of light offered by the night sky.

And this seemed to be enough; for now, her pale and heatless luster was sufficient to draw him, to allow himself to be drawn, to incite something real or imagined in his blood. "Abby," he said, moving toward her, feeling some vestigial pull when he spoke the name, the two rudimentary syllables that had once been so common on his lips. She looked at him as he drew near. Veiled by the dark, the hard specificity of the lines etched upon her face by recent days were all but erased.

"Why did you come today?" she said then before he could continue. Finally asking. Her tone was not harsh, not accusatory, but quietly demanding, deliberate.

He faltered. "I don't know," he answered, thinking of the terrible slackness on Levi's muddied face after he had fallen, the empty face looming under the beam of the flashlight like a moon in the dirt. He amended, "I can't really explain."

"Try."

He let out a breath of frustration. " I wish I could tell you."

"Then tell me."

"I can't. If you knew, you'd understand."

She was quiet, seeming to respect this response enough not to push again.

Then a softness fell into his voice. "But I did want to see you." He believed this now, though it might not have seemed true to him earlier. They stood side by side as he struggled to gather the effort to conquer his own resistance. And then, hastily, he put his arm around her in a way that he had not done since high school. He slipped his arm around her waist and pulled her toward him, almost roughly, and could feel through her thick jacket the once-familiar shape of her waist as she shivered against the wind. She did not resist, and he pulled her closer.

"You know," she said distantly, "even though the way he

went was terrible, how sudden it was, I still prefer it over the way you went. Just going silent for no reason, like you just checked out without telling me."

There was something pliant in her voice now, despite its distance. And with Abigail pressed to his side, Mark thought he could detect the current of his fate shifting again, merging now with hers and with the Gorskis'. Without even thinking he began to plot a future, one that seemed to unfurl before him upon the remainder of his life: he would learn to love Abigail again; he would father Zacharias's baby as his own; he would attend electrical school and buy them a house. He would make himself useful and productive. In his mind this was less a decision than a hard, lifelong indenture that he would accept without resistance, even gratefully.

"I'm sorry," he said.

"Are you?" she asked vaguely.

And with what seemed both impulse and a summoning of will, he pulled her to him full-on in the dark, then pressed his mouth blindly to hers, kissing her with a fervor that was hard and passionless and bitter, almost bludgeoning. She responded at first in kind, pressing back with empty abandon, but moments later he felt her mouth breaking up under his, suddenly going shapeless with grief. Even as he realized it was useless he clenched the back of her neck and continued to hold her to him, stubbornly, until she tore herself away in tears, grieving at last, her sobs ragged and guttural and bearing no resemblance to her crying during their fights long ago. There was nothing to say and he said nothing as she turned from him, as she retreated into the darkness, her sobbing figure going dim, then disappearing.

In the distance behind him, the door of the truck banged shut. The wind was skating hard over the surface of the water, agitating it into a jagged roil, and the river seemed wide and long and turbulent with life, destined to run and accumulate in endless and unthinking self-perpetuation. And Mark stood on its bank, quietly breathing. He saw nothing floating on the water now, no corpses, no specters. He saw only water drowning in water, minute perturbations collecting on a mass scale.

Overhead the stars looked on. Clustered along a galactic belt they now appeared not static but lazily adrift in ever-changing configuration, in a refusal to be schematized. And Mark thought, without believing, how each of those trillion dots had its own set of planets, its own revolving worlds. Without believing he thought of all the obscure forms of life that must be springing from their soil; he imagined shadowy figures standing on alien riverbanks in alien Pittsburghs, each bearing the terrible weight of some tiny murder—crimes and lives and lineages as ephemeral as a dream disintegrating with consciousness. He held to this thought, trying to siphon from it a breath of solace, but the image was too tenuous to sustain. As he stood by in the dark, his imagined counterparts seemed to recede from plausibility, to dwindle into the night, until finally there was only the river and the wind and the weight of Levi Gorski's murder, close and deafening and undeniable.

WHEN JOHNNY CAME SHUFFLING HOME

BY **K.C. CONSTANTINE**

McKees Rocks

Johnny Giumba graduated from high school on June 6, 1944, the same day the Allies invaded Normandy. A week later, he enlisted in the army, determined to kill Nips or Nazis—didn't matter which. All he needed was a gun and bullets. Everybody he knew said we needed to get them before they got us. Johnny agreed, at first. But then he remembered Pearl Harbor and he thought, they already got us, didn't they?

After basic training, he boarded a troop ship to England with an M1 Garand slung over his shoulder, just like everybody else aboard ship who wasn't a non-commissioned officer. But after training for a month in England, when he finally landed in France at the end of September, his first sergeant ordered everyone in his platoon to turn in their M-1s. Then they were all issued M1 carbines. Johnny didn't understand. Carbines were for the NCOs: staff sergeants, technical sergeants, master sergeants. Except for the NCOs in his platoon, nobody else was even a private first class.

His first sergeant told them not to worry about what kind of weapon they were carrying. The only Germans they were going to see would either be captured, wounded, or dead. They wouldn't have to shoot any of them. Then the first sergeant told them they were being reassigned to Graves Registration.

Johnny had never heard of Graves Registration. Neither had anyone else. He wanted to know what it was.

Don't worry, his first sergeant said. You'll find out soon enough.

His squad leader told them they were going to need their full field transport packs. Since all they'd done in France was stand around and wait, all they had to do was pick up their packs and put them on. Johnny wanted to know where they were going and what they were going to do when they got there.

We'll find out when we get there, his squad leader told him. There's a truck coming for us, he said. Other than that I don't know any more than you do.

They climbed into the back of the truck just as it was starting to rain. It rained the whole two hours the truck kept moving, never once getting up to more than twenty miles an hour. Sometimes the mud was up over the axles. Once they had to get out and push. Johnny and two of the others slipped and fell to their knees in the muck, and then got showered with mud as the tires finally got traction.

Just when Johnny thought he couldn't get wetter, muddier, or more miserable, he heard artillery. For the last few minutes or so, he'd been thinking it was thunder. He should've known it wasn't because he hadn't seen any lightning. And now the noise was growing sharper. Louder. More distinct. The explosions were coming in bursts of two, three, four, only seconds apart.

Johnny felt rumbling in his stomach. His throat was suddenly dry and felt like it was closing. It was getting harder to breathe. He was okay, he told himself. This stuff I'm feeling, it's just fear. Everybody's as scared as I am. They might not let on, but everybody's looking at where the sound of the explosions is coming from and nobody's saying anything.

Johnny'd felt the same way the time Billy Pristash talked him into going out on the river in his uncle's rowboat. He kept telling Johnny he was going to row straight into the wake of the sternwheeler that was heading downstream. At first, Johnny thought he was joking, but the more Johnny said he was crazy the more he laughed. That rooster-tail's ten feet high, Johnny said. You row into that it'll toss us around like a coupla corks. This boat will come down on our heads.

Billy said, That's the point, dummy. It's better'n Kenny-wood. Way more fun than the Racer or the Jack Rabbit. Especially cause that captain's looking right at us and any second now he's gonna blow the whistle. But that's all he can do. He knows we're gonna do it, and it's pissing him off real bad, but he can't do nothing but blow his whistle. Listen to him, there he goes, ha-ha! And here we go!

And there they went! Billy stroked fast as he could and rowed right into it, the crazy son of a bitch. And up and over they went, just like Johnny knew they would. Johnny dove left cause he didn't want to be under the boat when it flopped over to the right. The oars went flying like a coupla popsicle sticks, and Johnny got scared stiff cause he hadn't thought to take a big breath and didn't know which way was up and must've swallowed a quart of water. God knows what was in it.

Johnny finally popped to the surface, no thanks to himself. Just dumb luck. When they righted the rowboat and climbed in, Billy asked if Johnny had swallowed any Allegheny whitefish.

Never heard of that kind of fish, he replied.

Christ, you don't know nothing, do you? That's a rubber, dummy. They're all over the river. Probably swallowed a nigger fish too.

A what?

A turd, nitwit. Dumb as you are, I don't even know why I'm friends with you.

I'm not as dumb as you think, Johnny said. I only got two B's last year.

Two B's! Well goody for you! But that's school crap, it don't make you smart.

That's not what my dad says. Or my mom. They told me I keep getting grades like that, I could probably go to Carnegie Tech. Be an engineer.

An engineer! You go to Carnegie Tech so you can wind up driving a damn train? Boy, I heard everything now. We get back on the dirt, do me a favor. Pretend you don't know me.

Okay with me, Johnny said. 'Bout five minutes ago, I thought you were gonna kill us both.

Well are you dead now? Huh? Don't look dead to me. Hell, you don't even know when you're having fun. That was fun, dummy.

No it wasn't!

Aw, go home to your mommy and daddy. But don't forget what I said. From now on, you don't know me and I don't know you. Carnegie Tech. Christ Almighty.

Johnny remembered the conversation as though it had happened that morning, before he'd climbed up into the truck.

Fifteen minutes after they got to where they were going and were told what they were going to do and had started doing it, Johnny had already vomited twice. He was actually glad because retching made his eyes watery, so for a little while at least he couldn't really see what he was trying to pick up, trying to match up with other pieces and parts he'd already picked up. Then he vomited again. And again. All that came up the last time was saliva.

Every day was the same. Johnny woke up and marched

to the chow tent and tried to eat. As soon as he went out to start picking up the pieces, his breakfast came back up. He picked up more pieces. Tried to match them with still other pieces. Then they ate noon chow, and as soon as Johnny started work, the noon chow came back up. The vomiting got so bad, Johnny tried not to eat. But a day or so later, his squad leader caught on and ordered him to eat. Eat or die, his squad leader said. If you don't eat, eventually you die, everybody knows that. So Johnny tried to eat again. He tried hard. But nothing he put in his mouth would stay down. Or if it didn't come right back up, in a little while it would come out the other end, watery, until he was raw from wiping. Every time he swallowed he tasted acid. Then he started sniffling. He didn't know whether he had a cold or the flu or whether he was crying. His whole body ached like he had the flu. He had chills that made him shake. But he didn't have a fever. His nose wouldn't stop dripping. His eyes kept filling up with tears.

He wondered whether what was happening to him was happening to anybody else. When he looked around, the only thing he noticed was that nobody was looking anyone else in the eye. Everybody seemed to be slouching around, head down, trying to not see. Worse, it looked like they were trying to not be seen. The only guys who seemed to be talking, saying anything at all, were the NCOs who never left their bivouac area. And those guys didn't seem to have any trouble keeping their food down.

By the end of the second week, Johnny's pants were practically falling off him. He had to keep shortening his belt. At the end of three weeks, Johnny looked down at himself when he was trying to wash off the stench and saw that his stomach was sinking back toward his spine. His ribs were protruding. He caught a glimpse of himself in somebody else's metal mirror and he was so startled by the sight, he ran back to his sleeping bag and pulled it up over his head.

Johnny didn't know what to do, his life seemed so bleak. He thought and thought if there was anything he'd liked to do. And if there was, where did he like to do it? Back home? He couldn't remember where home was. He remembered a river he used to swim in. He also remembered he used to like arithmetic. Though when he tried to do simple addition or subtraction, he had to think really hard how to do it. But that turned out to be a good thing because thinking hard about how to add or subtract meant he could stop seeing, smelling, feeling what he did every day.

He soon tired of adding and subtracting. He tried dividing and multiplying. Over and over he multiplied time and then divided it. How many hours were in a month, how many minutes, how many seconds. He did the problems in the dirt with the point of his bayonet. He didn't have to look at anybody, nobody had to look at him. He didn't have to think about how skinny he was becoming. But in the middle of the third week he'd started to hallucinate. He saw a leg walking, hands clapping, a hand throwing a ball, a foot kicking a ball, teeth biting the air, lips spitting blood, brains thinking. When his first sergeant asked him what the fuck was going on with him, Johnny said, I'm seeing what thinking looks like.

Is that supposed to be funny? the first sergeant said.

Oh, it's no joke, Johnny said. It's hideous.

On his thirtieth day, seven hundred and twenty hours, forty-three thousand two hundred minutes, two million five hundred and ninety-two thousand seconds after he had been assigned to Graves Registration, on their first break of the morning, Johnny picked up his M-1 carbine, extracted the magazine to make sure it was fully loaded, reinserted the magazine, worked the bolt to put a round in the chamber, pushed the safety off, put the barrel in his mouth, and thought, here I am in the war and the only person I'm ever gonna shoot is me.

The next thing he knew, he was on his back and somebody was sitting on him, punching and pummeling him in the face, screaming.

His attacker kept shouting at him, You think you're gonna blow your fucking brains out and leave the rest of us here to stick your fucking dog tag in your teeth and hang the other one on your fucking carbine! You think you're gonna get out of this shit that easy? The fuck you are!

He didn't know who had knocked him down and beat him; he hadn't seen him coming. All he knew for sure was that he was having trouble breathing. He didn't know his nose had been smashed nearly flat. Blood was streaming into his eyes from the deep cuts on his eyebrows. Everything looked red. Some of his teeth had been knocked out. He was gagging on the blood pouring from his gums, trying not to swallow his teeth.

By the time he got to Paris, most of the swelling had gone down in his face. By the time he got to England, all the cuts had healed. By the time he got to Fort Dix, New Jersey, he wasn't wearing the straitjacket anymore, but he was still in handcuffs and leg irons.

A couple of months later, when the commanding officer of the prison ward in the hospital handed him his discharge papers, Johnny barely glanced at the words. Both of them said, *Unfit for Military Service*. Or maybe they said, *Unfit for Military Duty*. He wasn't sure. He was sure that he didn't care. He also didn't care that all the brass insignias had been removed from the new uniform he'd been issued. He didn't care that he had cash in his trouser pocket or that the corporal who'd handed him the cash had subtracted the price of a bus ticket back to Pittsburgh.

The last thing the prison ward CO said to him was, There's a VA hospital in Pittsburgh. Maybe they'll be able to help you there, son.

Johnny asked if he was supposed to report to that hospital.

No, the CO said, you're officially separated from the army, Mr. Giumba. I can't order you to report anywhere. I am advising you and suggesting strongly that you go there and ask for help because, son, you really need it.

The last thing they did before he got on the bus was remove the handcuffs and leg irons.

Sitting on the bench in the back of his parents' house on Washington Street in the McKees Rocks Bottoms, head back, eyes closed, the sun warm on his face, he wondered if anything would happen if he didn't go to that VA hospital, wherever it was. Since he was legally discharged, he was pretty sure they couldn't say he had deserted. They shot some guy in France for deserting.

He thought he'd keep wearing his uniform, even though he couldn't remember why he didn't have any insignias. He believed that if an MP showed up and tried to say he was a deserter, he could tell him the reason he was wearing his uniform was to show he was planning to go back. And if he was planning to go back that would mean he was not a deserter, just Absent Without Leave.

He read the discharge papers again. They said the same thing they said every time he'd read them. And five minutes later he couldn't remember whether it was Service or Duty he was unfit for.

When his mother and father were in the kitchen, they stopped talking when he passed through to go back to the bench outside. After he closed the door, he could hear them speaking, their voices low. Lately, it seemed every time he passed them, they were whispering. Another thing he noticed was they both were looking guilty. He wondered what they had done to look that way.

One afternoon his mother came to the door and said, How you feeling today, Johnny? You feeling any . . . different?

He shrugged. Just like he did every time she'd asked him that before.

Next question was as predictable as the last. You sure you don't want me to wash your clothes?

He shook his head no, closed his eyes, and lifted his face to the sun.

Her next comment had as little impact as the previous two. Johnny, don't get mad, but you're starting to smell.

He thought, starting? Jesus, you think I smell now? Should've smelled me a couple months ago. He didn't say it. There wasn't any point smarting off to his mother. She'd always been good to him. And anyway, none of what had happened since he'd arrived in France was her fault. Nothing was her fault. His father's either.

He started thinking about something he'd been thinking about for the last week or so. He'd been thinking about not talking anymore. But if he did stop talking, he worried his mother might think it was because she kept asking the same questions every day, and it wasn't that at all. It was just because he was running out of things to say and he was pretty sure that if he used up all his words talking about how he was or wasn't feeling or whether he did or didn't want his clothes washed, he might try to talk one day and find out all his words had been used up and he wouldn't be able to say anything else ever again because he was also pretty sure he didn't know where to go to get a supply of new words. Not new new words. Just words new to him. That, he felt sure, would be a real problem.

A big, poofy cloud hid the sun for a couple of minutes. Johnny took off his Ike jacket, hooked it over his shoulder, and started walking toward the river. He hadn't been down there since yesterday and he wanted to make sure it was still there. There was something about the river that soothed him. Maybe because one time he talked to some guy from the museum who was digging on the Indian Mound and that guy told him the river was real old. It had been there since the last glaciers melted. Thousands of years ago. At home that night Johnny multiplied how many hours, minutes, and seconds there were in a thousand years and he couldn't even pronounce the number he got. He did like the name of the river, although he'd had to ask his father what it was.

Ohio, his father said. It's the Ohio River. When you were a kid you used to go swimming in it, remember?

He wasn't sure if he could remember swimming in it. He did like the sound of the river's name. He walked around saying it over and over, singing it, sort of. Oh-high-oh.

It was unusually warm for November. Indian summer, his father said. He couldn't figure out why the summer would be named after the Indians. Maybe it was because of the Indian Mound, which was a little bit closer to Pittsburgh, where he talked to the guy from the museum who told him how old the river was. There were supposed to be a lot of Indians buried in that mound. Johnny believed that was true because he'd found a whole jarful of finger and toe bones. They were still on the shelf in his closet upstairs. Maybe when he went home he'd take them out of the jar and count them again. He wondered why finding those Indian bones had never bothered him, not anywhere near the way finding bones in France had bothered him. The pieces of bodies he collected in France made it impossible for him to eat, to nourish himself. In a month he'd lost nearly thirty pounds. A pound a day. When he was weighed in Fort Dix, he was so weak medics had to steady him on the scale.

A little before he reached the end of the block, he heard a horn and somebody calling his name. He kept walking at the same pace, but he thought he recognized the voice, so he turned and looked. The car was keeping pace with him. The driver was smiling.

Hey, Johnny boy, I heard you was home. Wasn't over there too long, huh?

Johnny stopped and bent over to get a better look at the driver. I know you?

Do you know me? The hell kinda question's 'at? I'm Billy. You don't remember me?

Billy?

Billy Pristash! The hell's the matter with you? You lose your mind?

No. I know where it is. He tapped his head. It's right up here.

Billy thought that was funny. You're jagging me, right?

Jagging you? I'm way over here, how could I be jagging you?

Oh, now I know you're jagging me. Hey, serious now, I wanna talk to you about something.

You said we were supposed to pretend we didn't know each other.

Ah, c'mon, man, that was a long time ago. My old lady talked to your old lady in church. Your old lady said you practically don't talk to nobody anymore. Says you just give everybody real short answers. Or else you don't say nothing.

Saying nothing, Johnny started walking again.

I guess you probably heard, Billy said. They tried to draft me last year, but I flunked the physical.

I heard something? What?

You didn't hear about me being 4-F?

Four what?

Four-F. You don't know what 4-F means?

No.

Well, before you hear some jagoff spreading rumors about me trying to beat the draft, I'm telling ya I flunked the physical. So you're hearing it right out of the horse's mouth. Something wrong with my heart. Some kinda murmur or some shit like 'at. So I'm 4-F. Unfit for military service.

That's what my discharge says. Or maybe it's duty I ain't fit for.

Billy threw his head back and laughed hard. He wiped his eyes. That's rich, he said. That's really rich. You and me. The same. Unfit.

No. Not the same.

No? How's come no?

You said I was dumb. You didn't know why you were friends with anybody dumb as me.

Aw, c'mon, Johnny, forget about that. That was a long time ago.

I remember like it was yesterday.

Aw, hey, man, I'm sorry I ever said anything like 'at, okay? Had it to do over, I would've never said it. So we're straight now, right?

Straight?

You know what I mean. Straight like friends again. Like we used to be. Like in junior high. Ninth grade.

You were in ninth. I was in eighth.

Okay, okay, so you was a year behind me. One year, what's the difference?

You never talked to me until now.

Ah, hey, you know, the conquering hero comes home, gotta talk to him, you know, that kinda shit.

Ain't a hero. Didn't conquer nobody.

Huh? You ain't? You didn't? See, right there, that's what I wanna talk to you about. What's it feel like, killing somebody? How many Krauts you kill?

None.

None? You didn't even kill one lousy Kraut? C'mon.

Not one.

C'mon, man, quit jagging me. Fuck were you doing over there?

Collecting garbage.

Collecting garbage?! Git outta here.

That's what war does. Makes garbage.

And that's what you were doing, huh? Picking up garbage, emptying cans, crap like 'at?

Johnny nodded.

Aw, quit jagging me, man, come on! This is me here. Billy.

Johnny turned away from the car and continued walking toward the river.

Hey! Where you going? I was just joking around, I didn't mean nothing.

Johnny kept walking, no faster, no slower.

Billy kept pace with him. Hey! Johnny! Wanna go for a ride? To where?

Anywhere, nowhere. C'mon, I'll show you my car. Just got it. Practically brand new. Only got twelve thousand miles on it. Not even that. Eleven nine five oh, to be exact. Bet you're wondering where I got the money, huh?

No. Ain't wondering.

You ain't? I'm gonna tell you anyway. Shit, man, I'm rolling in it. I'm driving a lift truck down the Wheel and Axel. They converted more than half the plant. Half's still making wheels and axles, the other half's making artillery shells. One oh five millimeters. Musta seen a lotta them over there, right?

No. I collected garbage.

Uh-huh. If you say so. Well, anyway, I'm getting all the overtime I want. I could work twelve hours every day if I wanted. And you know, everything over forty hours is time and a half. I paid cash for this baby. Only trouble is the gas rationing, you know?

No.

Yeah, well, how would you? They started last year. You're only allowed to buy so much a week, depending on what kinda job you got. I walk to work, so I'm only allowed, like, five gallons a week. Ain't much, but I know some guys, know what I mean? For the right price, the right people, whatever you want, you can get it. Hey, where you going? C'mon, get in. This baby can really go, it's a V8, you know?

No.

Well where you going anyway?

Oh-high-oh.

Ohio? You mean the river? Fuck you going there for?

To look. Makes me feel . . .

Makes you feel what?

Quiet.

Quiet?! Billy's face got pinched and wrinkly, like that was the stupidest thing he'd ever heard. For a long moment, he inched the car forward, not saying anything.

Hey, Johnny! Ho, Johnny! Hold up, man, I wanna ask you something, you know? I'm serious now.

Johnny stopped and looked over his shoulder at Billy.

What was it like, man, huh? I'm serious now. And don't bullshit me. You know. The war. Last couple guys I knew was over there, I asked them, but I know they was bullshitting me. I could tell, you know. They were trying really hard not to laugh at me. But I'm serious, man. I really wanna know.

Collected garbage.

Aw, come on, man, stop with that garbage shit. I wanna know what it was like. You can tell me.

I can?

Yeah. Cause we're straight now. Like before.

Nothing's like before. I collected—

C'mon, Johnny! Man, stop with the garbage shit.

Only person I ever tried to shoot was me.

Huh? You tried to kill yourself? What'd you wanna do that for?

Didn't wanna collect garbage no more.

Jesus Christ, you got a one-track mind, I'll say that for ya.

I like sitting on the tracks. I can watch the river.

One-track mind, I said, not railroad tracks. Thought I was gonna learn something talking to you. Turns out I was right all along. You really are fucking dumb.

Johnny stopped walking toward the river. He stepped out into the street. They were where Ella Street's bricks ran out, where it turned to dirt. Because it hadn't rained for more than a week, the dirt was a powdery grayish-tan dust. Johnny bent over from the waist.

He lowered his voice and talked evenly, not emphasizing anything. You wanna know? he said. You really wanna know what the war was like? Okay. I'll tell you. There was garbage. Everywhere. That's what the war was. Wasn't like anything. It was just garbage.

Oh, for Christ sake, stop it, willya?! You collected garbage. Maybe that's all you're good for. Don't know why I thought you was gonna give me the straight poop. From now on, it's gonna be just like before. Pretend you don't know me.

Johnny turned away from Billy and, stepping through the powdery dust, made his way across the Rox Boys Club baseball field. He walked past third base and through the grass of left field, hearing the cars and trucks humming above him on the McKees Rocks Bridge. He crossed the railroad tracks and slid down the bank of the Ohio to a small outcropping where he could sit and watch the greenish, grayish, brownish river flowing by. He felt better just thinking about how long this river had been flowing past where he was sitting and how much longer it would flow after he was dead. He thought of a song he'd heard one time.

Ol' man river, ol' man river, he don't know nothin', he don't say nothin', he jus' keeps rolling along.

Thinking those words made him feel even better.

I almost drowned in you once, he said. You damn near kept me down. But you didn't. Maybe I'd be better off if you had. I don't know how to think about that. But you got me for sure now. I'm gonna come here and look at you every day it's not raining or snowing hard. I'll do most of the talking. Sometimes I talk too much. A little while ago I almost told Billy Pristash a lotta stuff I said I was never gonna tell anybody. But I caught myself in time.

I didn't tell him, cause he would've blabbed everything I told him. But I can tell you. Cause like the song says, you don't know nothin', you don't say nothin', you jus' keep rollin' along.

It was a lot like here, Johnny said. Houses, apartment buildings, streets, gardens, trees, the river, factories, animals, cows, pigs, chickens, people. All blown to shit. All turned to garbage. Every day, every stinking day, and I do mean stinking, cause there ain't no stink like it in the whole world. When people die, when animals die, if nobody buries them, as soon as they die they start to rot. And when they start rotting, they give off all kinds of smells, there ain't any words for it, at least I don't have any words for it, all I know is it gets in your clothes, in your hair, in your mouth, in your nose, and no matter what you do, you can't get rid of it. And you think, the first time you smell it, what could be worse? Nothing could be worse than this. But there is something worse. It's called Graves Registration, a nice bullshit army term. And if you're unlucky enough to get put on GR, what you do every day as long as you can stand and bend over and zip and unzip body bags, you walk through wherever they drop you off, and you pick up bodies. And it ain't a picnic if the poor slob got dropped with one in the head or the heart, because the real hell is when you got to pick up the pieces of a whole lot of slobs that got hit by 88s. Cause that's when you have to walk around picking up heads, hair, brains, ears, eyeballs, noses, tongues, arms, legs, torsos—and that's if you can even make out what it is.

There's only one thing left I have to tell. Dog tags.

Everybody gets two. If you find a guy that died quick and in one piece, more or less, you open his mouth, you wedge one of his tags between his teeth and you take his rifle or carbine or whatever he was carrying and you put his bayonet on it and you stick it into the dirt beside him and you hang the other tag on his weapon someplace, wherever you can put it. Then you move on to the next one. Sometimes you have to use a rake and a shovel. And before you zip the bag, the last thing you do is write on the paper that goes with it, *A soldier known only to God.*

So now, Oh-high-oh, maybe you can tell why after thirty days of collecting that kinda thing, I wanted to blow the back of my head off. Didn't do it. Somebody knocked me down, beat the shit outta me. Smashed my nose, cut me all over my eyebrows, my cheeks. First time I saw a mirror, I looked at it and I said, Who is that? I really couldn't tell it was me. And so here I am, Oh-high-oh, I just dumped it all in you. Cause I can't carry it no more.

So far you haven't said anything. I don't think you'll blab no matter what I tell you. I'm pretty sure you won't. Not that I have anything else to say. I already told you the worst part.

A couple of hours later, Johnny stood and dusted off the seat of his trousers.

Then he stretched his arms up and said, See you, Oh-high-oh. Tomorrow, probably. Don't worry if I don't show up. Cause my dad and my mom, they're already worrying about what's gonna happen to me when they die. They think I don't hear them whispering about it. Bad as their hearing is, they have to talk loud, so it's easy to hear them. So, one day not too far down the road, I'm sure they'll throw their hands up and say they can't stand me anymore. Then they'll call the cops. And the cops will do what cops get paid to do. Take me to some nuthouse. Make sure I don't get loose.

I have to think of some way to make them understand I won't hold it against them for calling the cops. That won't be their fault, any more than any of the rest of this was ever their fault. Gonna be tough convincing them, though, cause no doubt they think I lost my mind, and as long as they think that they're never gonna believe anything I say. And anyway, I haven't lost my mind. I know right where it is. Same place it's always been. Under my hair.

Remember what I said, Oh-high-oh. Cause I've just decided I'm never gonna repeat it. Not to anybody. In fact, I might never say anything to anybody again.

PART III

UNIVERSITIES, PARKS, RECREATION

INTRUDER

BY Kathleen George

Schenley Farms

They were partners. One was white, one was black; they got along and liked working together. They'd come up through the ranks at the same time, slightly competitive, mostly friends.

The call came at one in the morning. All the good murders happened at night. The 911 operator told them, "Schenley Farms Terrace. A guy hit an intruder over the head. Called here, we sent the paramedics. They're saying the guy is dead. Patrol just got there."

"Breaking news," said Tolson, looking at his watch as he beckoned his partner down the stairs and outside to a fleet car. "Way too late for the eleven o'clock hash and nobody much watches the morning news, so we caught ourselves a break. I hate sounding dumb on the eleven o'clock news when we don't know what's happening."

"You can manage to sound dumb anytime," Paulson said. Tolson shot him a look and then Paulson laughed and asked, "Okay, what is it?"

"Manslaughter, probably." Tolson gave the few details he had while he radioed patrol to call him on his cell.

Damion Paulson drove them, expertly shooting to the parkway and then passing everybody on the road.

Tolson's phone rang, speaker on. The patrol cop had five minutes on them. "Anything you can tell us?"

"He's dead. Mashed-up head and lots of blood. Man, he must've got hit hard. Family is all upset. Everybody is shaking and crying. They have accents. I don't know what kind. They're foreigners."

"Okay. What else?" Tolson asked.

"The daughter. She's something else. She looks like some kind of movie star. Like maybe Indian or something, but with light eyes. Maybe she's somebody famous, I don't know."

Paulson was laughing silently.

"Anything else about the homicide?" Tolson pressed.

"Not yet. Just everybody's upset. They're talking in their language."

Tolson hung up. "Check your prejudice at the door," he quipped. He was serious, though. Now was not the time to fuck up. *Respectful to foreigners* was drummed into their heads. Also other lessons: *Poor doesn't mean dumb. Every poor dead son of a bitch was a human being.*

"You ever hang around Schenley Farms?" Tolson asked Paulson, who had grown up near there, in the Hill District.

"Nah."

Schenley Farms, they knew, had some fancy properties, but the fanciest mansions were closer to Oakland. Old money as well as some high brass from the universities resided there. Then there were the somewhat fancy houses on the steeper streets of Schenley Farms, and then way up above them was the beginning of "the hill," a black ghetto. Five minutes later they were at the house. It was far from shabby.

A couple of TV news trucks were parked on the street. Tolson told reporters he passed, walking to the house, "We'll have a statement for you in thirty minutes." They went inside.

The inside of the house was super fancy. Glass, white, glass, white. Plush carpets. Tolson knew they were bringing in dirt and he felt uncomfortable. It was late May and the earth was moist. The patrol cop said, "Down here," and led them down a set of carpeted steps to a finished basement that was basically a well decked-out apartment. The paramedics were standing around like oafs. The guy on the floor of this downstairs apartment was so totally dead—extreme measures definitely not necessary. He was a black guy, and they could see that he was wearing running shoes, jeans, and a T-shirt of a good quality, nice-looking things. A pocketknife lay near the body.

Tolson and Paulson moved outside the basement door. They examined the grounds, the shaved bits of door around the lock, then came back in and looked around. Cushy, cushy sofas and a huge TV. Tolson walked around, Paulson behind him, briefly taking in the little kitchen and the bathroom, all very state of the art.

"You know how much that kind of shower setup costs?" Paulson asked. He was married and trying to renovate a house. "And the faucets. Way out of my range."

"Pretty," Tolson admitted. "Pretty stuff, all right." He was not married. He had just suffered a breakup and was nursing a broken heart. He hadn't even known she was unhappy. She'd told him that was because he wasn't too smart.

They checked the victim for ID. There was nothing in his pockets. "This knife was just like this?"

The patrol cop told them it was.

Had the deceased dropped it that way when he fell? Odd.

They headed upstairs to talk to the family.

They tiptoed through the huge living room with its two levels to where the patrol cop pointed them, saying, "They told me they'd be in the kitchen."

The kitchen was not exactly a kitchen. It was perhaps

larger than the two-tiered living room. Its paned glass windows looked clean even by night, the paint on the wood perfect. It had clearly been added onto the house, using up part of the yard. It had a fireplace and a seating area with comfortable chairs, like a second living room. In a gazebo kind of thing at one end was a dining table and chairs. There were windows everywhere. These cats were in favor of windows. One arched window at the dining end looked out onto the hillside where outdoor lights showed there were terraced levels, all planted with colorful flowers—the slope was landscaped to within an inch of its life.

The dining table was glass too. Light. Light everywhere.

The detectives turned away from the view to find the family huddled in the back near the cooking area, comforting a young woman. They broke apart reluctantly to come forward. The father indicated the glass dining table, which seated eight.

Tolson said, "Fine. Yes, let's sit there. We need to ask you some questions." Five family members trooped in front of the detectives. They appeared to be father, mother, sister, brother, grandmother, four of them huddling protectively over the fifth, the girl, so that at first the detectives couldn't see her.

When they all got to the table where the family took separate seats, Tolson and Paulson got their first look at her.

She was the most beautiful woman Tolson had ever laid eyes on. She was like Elizabeth Taylor in her youth in those old, old movies—light eyes, dark hair, and lips, skin, that made his heart stop. She held a cloth to the side of her face.

"You're hurt?"

She shook her head.

The father said firmly, "He hit her. The guy hit her."

"Should you have medical help?"

She shook her head. Her brother sat next to her at the table but his shoulders were angled away from her—distancing himself for some reason.

Maybe she *was* famous, an actress or something—everything she did, even the way she shook her head, seemed watchable and interesting.

"I'm Detective Tolson, this is Detective Paulson. We'll want your names. And then the whole story, from the beginning."

The father's name was Yousef, the son Javeed. The old baba, the mother's mother, was Fatemeh, the mother was Malakeh, and the girl was Azita. The last name of the family was Samadi. Tolson laboriously copied these into his book and checked the spelling by reading each name back.

"This is your home? You live here?"

Everybody looked to Yousef Samadi, who answered. "Most of the year."

"What does that mean?"

"We have other homes. We travel. I travel a lot," Yousef explained, "but the children are in school so mostly they are here."

"We went to Florida in January," the son added.

"Oh, you mean a vacation?"

"A trip," Samadi said. "I had some business there. I made sure they did their schoolwork. We have a home there."

"You said homes? I suppose I should get it all down. Somewhere else?"

"Yes. In Iran, of course. Our main home. And we have an apartment in Paris."

"I see," Tolson said. "Would someone write the addresses for us? To make all this go quicker?"

Javeed volunteered to do that.

Tolson asked Yousef, "Your work is here?"

"I have several businesses. Not here, but I can work here by phone and computer."

"What kind of business do you do?"

"Import."

"I see." Dope, guns, trinkets, antiques? "What products?"

"Carpets, rugs, beautiful things."

Tolson nodded and turned to Paulson to bring him into the questioning phase. "Anything?"

Paulson said, "We'll need to hear from the beginning what happened tonight."

"Right," Tolson said. "Go ahead."

"We were in bed," Yousef began. "The women were sleeping. They didn't hear anything. Javeed was in his room. I thought he was asleep. But he was listening to something—" He made a gesture to his ears to indicate contempt toward MP3 players. "So he still didn't hear. I was in my bed. I was watching my television. I thought I heard a sound. High-pitched. A voice. From the recreation room. I thought maybe an intruder, maybe a robber got hurt. But I knew sometimes my daughter went down there late, watching TV and doing her homework at the same time. I had to go down sometimes in the middle of the night to tell her to go to bed." He looked around at his family. They nodded at him, some almost imperceptibly.

A knock at the front door and a simultaneous call on the police radio interrupted Samadi's narrative.

"We're here," a crackling voice came through on the radio.

"What's happening? Who is that?" Samadi held a hand over his heart.

"Our team. We have to get prints, photos."

Azita put her hands over her face. Her brother nudged her. He said something like, "You might have to."

Tolson saw a nasty bruise on her cheekbone near her ear.

Detective Paulson went to the door to let in the forensics team. Tolson got up too, to see who had been sent. Lucky. They'd got the best lab guys. He indicated the basement where the team should go. Then he and Paulson headed back to their seats.

"Why won't they take the man away?" the wife was murmuring to her husband. "And the blood? I won't ever go down there again. I want to move."

"Let's be patient," Samadi said. "Let's find out how they do it. They're professionals." He was an imposing man, not just because he was well-barbered and distinguished looking, but also because it was clear he was used to exercising his will.

Tolson answered formally. "We'll tape the room off. When we have all the evidence we need, a team will come in and clean up. We can give you some names of experts at cleanup. You might want to change the carpet simply because . . . because you want to change it. But that's to be decided by you later."

Azita had begun crying.

"What is it?" Paulson asked.

"A man died in our house. It makes me feel . . . unlucky."

"Unlucky?"

"And sad."

"You were down there when he broke in?"

"Oh, yes."

"You didn't hear him breaking in?"

"I had fallen asleep. The TV was on."

"I see. And then?"

"Something woke me. And I saw him. And I made a sound. And my father came down. When he saw the man he grabbed a baseball bat."

"There was a bat there?"

"The whole corner," Yousef interrupted. "You saw it. Sports equipment. I didn't think; I couldn't think. I wanted something that would be . . . far from my body and strong. I wanted to save my daughter."

"Save her?"

"He was holding her. He had a knife."

"We saw the knife," Paulson volunteered. "Beside the body."

Tolson said, "So, you wanted distance from him as you hit him. But you, Azita, were in the man's grip. There's no blood on you. How is that?"

"There was." She shuddered. "I showered. I changed clothes."

"I see. Where are the clothes you were wearing?"

"In the garbage. My mother took them."

"We're going to need them," Paulson said kindly. "You can't do that. You can't make those decisions. They're evidence. Out back?"

The mother glanced at her husband, then nodded.

"I'll tell the techs to get them," Paulson said, again very gently.

Tolson asked, "How long before you called us?"

"Right away."

"But the shower? Your daughter had a shower?"

"Maybe I sat with her for a few minutes to calm her, I don't remember. There's a shower in the basement. She used that."

"The change of clothes?"

"My wife brought her fresh clothes."

"We need to go to your living room and reenact. You should show us where you were at each point. But first, did you *know* the young man? Any of you?"

They all said no.

"Are you sure? Did you all look at him?"

"We didn't let Javeed or my mother-in-law go down to look, but my wife and I saw him. He was not familiar."

"Azita?"

"Please, no."

"What?"

"I didn't know him."

"Did the man speak? What did he say to you?"

She hesitated.

"Azita?" her father prompted.

"He said, 'I need jewels, money, cash, lots of cash, now.' I said, 'I can get you a little cash.' But I made a noise. He hit me. He said, 'Shut up or I'll kill you.' He pulled a knife. I kept talking, telling him we had some cash on hand, not much, but that I would find him something else of value. Then my father came down. The surprise made him . . . the man . . . turn from me. Then he turned back because . . . I don't know, maybe he was going to stab me. My father hit him."

"How many times?"

"Two."

"Please promise me," Yousef Samadi said suddenly, "that you will keep this out of the papers and the news."

Tolson paused and looked at him, surprised. "There is no way I can do that. We have freedom of the press."

"Please. Keep my daughter out of it. She's young. She's still in high school. Don't you understand that? Please."

"I'll do my best on that end."

The father sighed heavily.

They went into the living room and played out the scenario the girl had described—sleep, sound of break-in, scream, words of threat, knife pulled, father arrives, hit to the head.

They played it a couple of times while the techs worked in the basement room. Azita did it beautifully. She turned like a dancer, got up off the sofa like a princess awaking from sleep in a Disney film.

After they'd seen the act, Tolson went outside to talk to the news folks who had gathered and were sitting in open cars, smoking and chatting amongst themselves. Paulson stood in the doorway. Tolson said simply, "The apparent situation is that an intruder broke into the basement of this home. The owner who was upstairs alleges that he was alerted by a sound. He went downstairs. The man made threats to his family. The owner hit the man and the blow killed him. The intruder is as yet unidentified. We are working on an identification and checking all aspects of the case."

Tolson and Paulson went back inside. "We'll probably be here until about dawn," they told the family.

"Why?"

"Everything takes time. The techs need time. Also, we'll need to get DNA and fingerprints from you."

"From us?"

"Yes."

"Is this normal?" Samadi asked. He drew himself up. "Is this because we are Iranian?"

"Not because you are Iranian. It's normal practice. We need to corroborate your account so you don't get in trouble. Please don't worry," Paulson said in his honey voice. "This will soon be in the past."

The atmosphere softened a bit after that. The grandmother yawned and slept in a chair. The family made toast, but then started to forage for larger items of food from the fridge. "What can I prepare for you?" the mother asked the detectives.

The partners managed to refuse her offer of food and

drink, but they sent a patrol cop to Ritter's to pick up middle-of-the-night sandwiches for themselves and the techs.

After they finished taking DNA swabs and fingerprints, they allowed the family to go to bed, all except Yousef, who more than agreed to be the point person. "I don't sleep much anyway," he said.

"Why is that?"

"Arthritis, gout, business worries."

"I'm curious. Why did you choose Schenley Farms?" Paulson asked. "I mean, of all the places in the city. Foreign visitors seem to like living in the suburbs."

"My wife teaches at CMU."

"She's a professor?" Paulson didn't hide his surprise very well.

"Yes. Fairly famous."

"What subject?"

"Business."

There. They'd made a gaff. Assumed the wife was a stay-at-home because she looked a certain polite way and didn't mouth off.

The next day they got an ID on the intruder. He was Jacob Wilson. He'd been in trouble before, for drugs. He'd lived in the Hill District. They went to see his mother and delivered the bad news.

She took it like a soldier, very strong. She provided pictures of Jacob, and when the cops could see his face and the structure of his very fine skull, they saw he'd been an extremely good-looking guy. He'd been twenty-three years old. His mother said, "I knew he had some trouble awhile back. He went to meetings. He got clean twice. He . . . must have backslid, I guess. I didn't think so, but I guess he did. If I tell you he was a good kid, you won't believe me, but he was. He was an addict but not a criminal. He was an innocent boy, all his life. An innocent."

"Who were some of his friends?" Paulson asked. "We'd like to talk to them."

Lila Wilson, not crying, but clearly in a deep sadness that took her voice down to a whisper, gave the names of two young men who might have seen her son in recent weeks.

The detectives went to their car. They sat for a moment.

"Nice lady," Tolson said.

"Why are we still looking into this?"

"Tie up the ends. Be sure."

"Right. Right. Here's what I'm thinking. If I met Azita when I was younger . . ."

"She might like them older."

"Younger than I am now . . . You know what I mean."

"Right. That's why we're looking."

Wilson's friends were not that easy to track down. Finally, the detectives caught up with one of them, Pierre Smith, who told them where the second friend, Joe Sandusky, could probably be found. Pierre, looking at the pictures of first Yousef, then of Javeed, then of Azita, said no, he'd never seen them or heard of them. "Wouldn't mind knowing the girl," he said wide-eyed.

The other friend, Joe Sandusky, didn't recognize the photos either. When asked about his friend, he said it was a terrible tragedy and that he didn't believe the crap about Jacob breaking into a house. "Maybe he had a hookup with the chick. He liked women."

"How would we find out if he knew her?"

"Beats me."

"Tell us where the hangout was. Where he bought stuff. Where he might have met her."

"What you talking about?"

"I think you know," said Paulson. "Drugs. Recreational drugs."

"I don't know about any of that."

"You want to be obstructing an investigation?"

"Nope."

"You want to think again? Place where the high school kids buy their stuff."

"Upper Craig Street." He gave a number. "Maybe there. You're going to pin the blame on Jacob no matter what. This sucks."

"His mother told us he was backsliding. What was he on?"

"Just weed. Just fucking weed. He stopped messing with the other stuff."

"Ecstasy?"

"Maybe sometimes."

The owner of the apartment on Craig was Amsel Dickens, a big, muscular African American. "I ain't answering anything," he said.

"We don't want to bust you for the weed. We don't care about the weed. The E. Any of that. Just want to show you a picture. Ever seen this boy?"

"Nah."

"This girl?"

"No."

"Willing to take a lie detector?"

"Yeah, sure."

"Look again. What about this guy?"

"Yeah. Now I see him, yeah."

"He buy much?"

"Not too much."

"You see a lot of him?"

"No."

"Okay. Look at the girl again."

Amsel looked hard, extra hard, as if it took awhile to study her face, as if she was plain and unmemorable. Tolson switched the picture they'd taken of Azita with her wounded cheek with another photo, her high school glamour shot—not that she looked shabby in the police photo. Amsel kept studying, looking this way and that.

"I'll take that as a yes," Tolson said.

"We're going to end up not having any proof," Paulson said when they were back in the fleet car.

"When did you get the feeling we were had?"

"Today. Breakfast, I was thinking, let them go, you know, the man was defending his house—but then I saw Wilson's picture and I got a whole 'nother story going in my head."

"You think race comes into it?"

"When does race not come into it?"

"I don't know."

"By now this Samadi's lawyered up, I bet."

"I'd say."

"Cause we took the DNA. He didn't like that."

"He was believable. Very believable. Shaking and all. Maybe everything he said was true."

"Maybe, yeah. We don't want to be prejudiced." Paulson smiled.

"Are we jumping on them?"

"Because they want to nuke the world? Because they have four houses and I can't afford faucets for my one? I'm thinking it through."

* * *

Later that day some results came in. They asked Mr. Samadi to come up to the office. They thought he would have a lawyer with him and were surprised that he didn't. They sat with him in a nonthreatening meeting room and said, "Seems you hit the victim three times."

"Did I?"

"All from behind."

"I can't remember. It's a blur."

"You were upset."

"What man in his right mind wouldn't be?"

"The knife had your prints on it, his prints on it. They were overlapping, like his then yours, then his, in that order. Can you tell us about that?"

"I did move the knife. He dropped it when I hit him and I shouldn't have moved it, but I did—I put it near the body."

"I see," said Tolson. "So you were the last one to touch it?"

"I think so. I don't remember. I was very upset."

"The scenario we saw was not totally complete?"

"Look. What are you doing? I was protecting my property. I know enough about this country to know I have a right to that."

"Your daughter's fingerprints were on the man's belt buckle."

There was a long silence.

"I don't know each move. She was defending herself. I'm sure she pushed."

"What will you tell us about her DNA being found on the guy?" Everything stopped. Samadi froze momentarily. Tolson was police-tricking. The DNA hadn't been tested yet. It would take weeks. His phrasing, he thought, was clever. He never said it *was* there, only asked what Samadi would say.

"If you had a beautiful daughter and she was being raped, what would you do?"

"Why didn't you tell us that before?"

"Scum run the news here. That's what you do in this country. American scum know nothing about a girl's reputation, her honor. This is not something to broadcast."

"Had he already raped her?"

"No. He had a knife. He had her clothes half off. He was holding the knife to her head and making her . . . kneel in front of him."

They ran the questions a couple more times for consistency. "How about we take a polygraph and be done with this?"

"I think . . . I think I will consult a lawyer. I do not wish to be treated this way."

After Samadi left, Paulson said, "I do have a beautiful daughter and if she was a teenager, I might lose it in a situation like that. I would try not to. But I might not be able to help myself."

"Three times? From behind?" Tolson was never sure in the devil's advocate game they played which one of them would take up which argument. This time they switched back and forth, each playing both "nuke the guy" and "foreign prince defends honor."

"Maybe two."

It took time.

Tolson's personal life made a deeper dive in the interim. He tried to contact Jenna. She told him to get lost.

Meanwhile, they kept an eye on the drug house. They attended the Wilson boy's funeral and talked to neighbors, school chums—everyone said Jacob was a sweet boy, not a criminal of any sort, just sometimes depressed. No job, hadn't liked school, worked here and there, and got down on himself. He was handsome so he relied on that to pick himself up. Women. Adoration. Being loved. And that usually led to sadness because they invariably decided he had nothing to offer them.

"Hmph," said Tolson.

Paulson said, "I feel for that kid. That could have been me if I hadn't got it together."

"You're not so handsome. This kid was handsome." Tolson grinned.

In the next week, they called neighbors at the Florida address. The telephone work was time consuming and seemed to go nowhere for days, but eventually they learned that the family had actually enrolled the kids in school last January. That was a little odd. It took them forever to find the school. The principal, when she answered, said, "Yes, I remember. I thought the children were charming. The girl was a stunner. But then the family whisked them out of school."

Tolson put the call on speakerphone so his partner could participate. He asked, "You know why they didn't stay in school? I mean, why start and stop?"

She hesitated. "I don't want to say anything untrue."

"Well, what part do you know?"

"I think . . . the father thought the girl was going wild."

"Was she?"

"I don't know. As far as I'm concerned, if I looked like that, I would have a royal good time. Why shouldn't women have the same chances to play that men do?"

"I totally agree," Paulson put in. "This is Detective Paulson here. I know a lot of men who don't agree, but I'm ready to say they have that right. She was what? Sixteen?"

"I think so. Yes, sixteen."

When they ended the call, Tolson said, "You speak with a forked tongue."

"How so?"

"Aren't you the guy who said you'd kill anybody messing with your daughter?"

"Right. Various codes. What other girls can do, what your own daughter can do. Also what's not okay to do under the age of thirty-five. After thirty-five, they're on their own. If you ever have a daughter, you'll understand."

Tolson shook his head. "Well, let's call the Frenchies."

The conversation with the foreign officer started out pretty well in pidgin French and pidgin English. But the questions they needed to ask were too complex to continue. They eventually had to stop at wishing each other well and sending mutual respect across the ocean.

Another couple of weeks went by. The DNA test results came in. Most of it confirmed who touched the knife, who touched the bat, who touched the belt. But there was additional information. Azita's DNA was everywhere, on the guy's mouth, cheeks, neck, chest, and yes, his penis. It didn't form a picture of a forced encounter.

They called Samadi's lawyer and set the polygraph for two days hence, rehearsing the questions that might shake the guy's story.

And then they had some luck. They drove to the drug house the next day when school was letting out, and, though they expected nothing, really expected nothing, they got a bit of something. Azita, followed by two eager boys, was going into the house.

"She doesn't look too upset or sad these days," Paulson observed.

"No. If she knew the guy, why would none of her friends come forward? Say something?"

But they both knew she had some sort of magical power. You wanted to protect her, you wanted to be loved by her.

About ten minutes went by while they talked about what they would ask when she emerged. But she didn't come out. Finally, they idled the car forward, parked, and went to the door.

"Who is it?"

"It's us. Detectives Paulson and Tolson. Just want to talk to Amsel, briefly, outside. No arrests."

The door opened slowly and Amsel slipped outside, holding a set of keys.

"The girl. The one you didn't know. Do you recognize her from this picture now?" Tolson pulled out the glamour photo.

"Yeah. What? Am I under arrest?"

"Not if you tell the truth. What's she doing in there?"

"She has a boyfriend. She's just hanging with him."

"Front room, back room?"

Amsel looked at them with hard eyes. "You guys are creeps. She's in the back room, okay?"

"Was she ever in the back room with this other guy?" Tolson pulled out the other photo, now getting worn from sitting at the back of his notepad.

"Yes. Yes."

"He was her boyfriend?"

"Yes. Am I under arrest?"

"No, you're cool. Just let us in. We'll talk to her. Her father is going to want her home soon."

Amsel dangled the keys. He looked terrified. "Okay," he said, and he let them in.

Tolson felt like a creep.

Paulson tapped lightly on the bedroom door. "Azita Samadi. We need to talk to you."

Tolson felt oddly frightened in a way he hadn't before. Of the girl. Of her father.

Azita came out of the room. She was disheveled, her eyes defiant. She was breathtaking. "What do you want with me?"

"Just . . . a talk."

"I have a right to a life."

"Come to the car. We'll talk in the car."

"Will you be feeling me up?"

"No. No, we won't be doing that."

The two detectives tried to walk casually to the car so as not to excite any trouble, though Tolson edged a little in front so she wouldn't run. Somebody pretty soon had to start telling the truth. They put her in the passenger seat. Paulson sat in front with her and Tolson climbed in back. He nodded to Paulson to start. He was figuring out how he wanted to do this.

"Here's the part we know," Paulson said. "You have boyfriends. That's your business. You like to smoke weed. We're not going to bother you about weed. At one point Jacob Wilson was your boyfriend. So you don't have to deny any of that. You can just say yes."

"So?"

"So he's dead."

There was a long silence. Tolson added after a while, "We're told he was a young man who didn't quite know himself. Maybe he went after women who were too young. That's not good. But we don't know that he did anything he should have died for. We're told he was gentle. Is that true?"

Some of her fight was gone. "Yes."

"Did he rape you? We're going to need to do a lie detector, so you might as well tell the truth."

"No."

"Did he try to?"

"No."

"Did he pull a knife on you?"

"No."

"Had you had sex with him before?"

Defiant again, she said, "Yes. What of it?"

"He died. He's dead."

Her hand went to her mouth and she started to cry. She did it very beautifully again. Tolson wanted to touch her. Paulson said, "Why would your father think it was a rape? Did you cry rape to save yourself from your father's anger?"

"I didn't say anything. He was there with the bat before I knew what was happening."

"And then he messed with the lock and the knife."

She swiped at her eyes and seemed as if she would not answer. "Yes."

"We have to do right by Jacob Wilson."

She nodded. "He was sweet. Not too savvy but very sweet. I love my father. What's going to happen to him?"

"He's going to go to jail," Tolson said. He was glad she was finally talking.

"For sure?"

"He has a good lawyer, he'll probably get a short sentence. A jury will be sympathetic that he was acting by some code he thought was right."

"What a mess. For all of us."

Tolson couldn't let up. He wanted to hear her talk. "You might have some hard times. The money won't flow in if your pop is in jail."

She smiled. "Pop. It's such a funny word. I'm not worried about that. My mother pretty much does everything anyway."

"Oh?"

"So you'll be free for a while," Paulson said. He sounded sad and mad.

"And so we have to do what we have to do," Tolson said. "Where's your father now? Back at the house?"

She smiled. "He's in Iran."

"Huh?"

"He left yesterday." She looked at them straight on. "Of course. What did you think?"

"He can't just do that."

"He can. Believe me."

Tolson tried to think what he wanted to ask her. He wanted her to be different, to say something different.

She got out of the car and started walking toward home. She walked smoothly and confidently. They saw her pull out a cell phone. It seemed she punched in a lot of numbers before she started speaking.

They just kept looking until she was out of sight.

LOADED

BY REBECCA DRAKE

Fox Chapel

It rained on moving day, quarter-size drops splashing like bloodstains on the stone walkway. The movers cursed under their breaths and one of them slipped as they were carrying in an antique sideboard. The heavy end left his blunt hands, landing with a crash that chipped the mahogany veneer.

Andrew watched from the doorway of the house, relieved that the damage was on the left side. Given its placement in the dining room, Christine would be unlikely to notice.

She had a tendency to overreact and he imagined if she'd been the one to see the accident she would have yelled at the movers and they might have abandoned the job half-done, a trail of possessions left on the front lawn to soak up the rain.

Luckily, she'd been out of earshot, down the hall in what was to be the boys' bedroom, picking paint colors with her mother.

It was their first house. She made him lift her over the threshold in full view of her parents and the movers. He'd done the same thing in their apartment six years earlier, just a week after their wedding, tired and tanned from their honeymoon in Aruba, both of them laughing as he'd hoisted her into his arms and swung her through the narrow doorway.

Six years later he felt embarrassed and a little annoyed. Things were different between them. Christine was noticeably heavier, for starters, carrying twenty extra pounds of baby weight, which no one was supposed to mention even though their younger son was six months old. "You look so good!" all her friends said, as if there was some unwritten female rule to lie about physical appearance.

She'd giggled as he hoisted her into his arms and he'd forced a smile. Out of the corner of his eye he'd seen one of the movers, a young man with heavily tattooed arms, staring at him with a hardened expression while smoking a cigarette. Andrew had flushed and looked away, but not before seeing the man toss the cigarette onto the lawn. His lawn.

He hadn't wanted to buy a house. They'd spent six years in a duplex in the East End and he'd been happy there, able to walk to the university or stop for milk on his way home, just a few blocks to meet friends for a drink in the evening. It met all his needs, until the convenience store got robbed in broad daylight, and a neighbor was mugged, and the lawn chairs disappeared. Christine started saying that she didn't feel safe. She talked about moving out of the city and said it was better for kids. When she got pregnant with their second son, Andrew knew his days in the city were numbered.

Fox Chapel was too expensive for them, but Christine refused to look farther out, arguing that it had good schools and they'd be close to her parents. Not an incentive for Andrew, but after six years of marriage he'd learned when to shut up.

In their price bracket, they were stuck looking at fixer-uppers, which meant 1960s-era ranches or early-'70s faux colonials, with avocado kitchens and baths, and basement rec rooms. The house they settled on—a four-bedroom with potential—had a red Naugahyde bar in the basement. Andrew pictured himself standing behind it and offering his friends martinis. It was so retro it was almost hip. Almost. He felt panicky.

Their realtor, an older brittle blonde with orangish skin named Tippy Cooperman, looked right at home sidling up to the bar. "You'll have lots of fun down here!" she brayed, smacking the black Formica counter.

She turned every criticism of the house into something positive. So when Andrew noticed that it needed new windows, Tippy said, "Look at all that natural light!" As for the overgrown, bushy two-acre lot, she said, "Such an excellent deal for all this land!" She pushed them to make an offer, saying it was a great investment.

The only investment Andrew could focus on was the time it would take to get the house and yard into shape. Christine looked at the larger homes surrounding them and agreed with Tippy. Apparently, her father agreed too, because the next day, after they'd been out to see it with their daughter, his in-laws offered to give them the down payment and cover the closing costs.

"It's a good starter home," Donald Wallace declared after he'd walked through it. He was a large, ruddy-cheeked businessman with a full head of silvery white hair, who'd amassed a fortune by tripling the size of his grandfather's plumbing supply company. Semiretired, he spent his days staring at a flat screen in his enormous home or playing endless rounds of golf at the country club. He was the sort of man who distrusted academia and thought even less of scientists. When Andrew couldn't easily sum up his research in physics, it was immediately suspect.

Donald's small, plump wife, Joyce, bustled about on moving day, watching over the grandkids and helping Christine direct the placement of furniture. Smiling, she told Andrew that "of course" she and Donald would ensure they got invited to join the country club.

That night, their first in the new house, they lay in bed in their master bedroom suite, which was painted a bilious shade of blue. Christine whispered, "Can you believe it? We're homeowners!" She sounded elated. He felt only panic: his life was over; he was thirty-two years old.

Startled awake at three by Sam's high-pitched crying, Andrew shot up in bed and didn't recognize the room. Christine didn't stir, a lump under the sheets, her dark hair falling in lank, sweaty strands across the pillow.

He let her sleep, stumbling from their room and padding along the dark, unfamiliar hallway to the boys' bedroom. Three-year-old Henry slept in his new bed, looking smaller than he had in the crib that was now Sam's, oblivious to his younger brother's wailing. A nightlight in the shape of a cartoon dinosaur cast a soft yellow glow.

Sam stopped crying for a few seconds when he saw his father looming above him and then started up again. It reminded Andrew of an air raid siren. "Hush now, little guy," he whispered, scooping him up and heading into the kitchen.

Christine pumped so that Andrew wouldn't "miss out" on feedings. He took one of the bottles from the fridge and warmed it, letting his son gnaw rodent-like on one of his fingers while they waited.

Sam nursed voraciously, cupping the bottle with small hands and sucking down the milk like the final beer at last call.

The night was stifling. Andrew carried Sam and the bottle out onto the back deck, quietly sliding open the screen door. The weathered wood felt cool under his feet. The air throbbed with locusts and crickets. The leafy branches of looming oak and maple trees formed a canopy over their heads, and beyond them, luminous and large, the stars. Movement caught his eye and he turned to see a woman standing on the back deck of the house closest to theirs, which wasn't close, not by city standards. She was naked, her skin glowing white in the moonlight. Her long, straight hair looked like liquid silver. As he watched she raised her hands above her head, pressing them together and arching her long, lean body back. Yoga at three in the morning.

He stood in the shadows and watched, wondering if she knew he was there. A few minutes of stretching and a man suddenly appeared behind her. It was too far away to hear anything, but Andrew clearly saw the guy wrap his hand in that long silver hair and pull. She moved with her hair, a single cry of pain loud enough to echo through the trees. It could have been a cat or a bird; no one would investigate. Sam paused in his guzzling, the bottle popping free of his milky lips, and stirred in his father's arms.

Andrew stood still, afraid to move, unable to turn away. The couple tussled silently for a minute, the man letting go of her hair, but only to move his hand to her upper arm. He dragged her into their house. Andrew stood there a moment longer on shaky legs, his breathing rough and fast in his ears. The clatter of the bottle falling onto the deck startled him— Sam had fallen asleep in his arms.

On the following Friday, they invited friends from the city out to visit their new house. Christine's idea. They would grill, and everyone could sit on the back deck and admire the view.

"Hey, Soccer Dad," Jason teased, accepting the beer that Andrew pulled from the fridge. "When are you getting the minivan and the golden retriever?"

"Ha fucking ha." Andrew pulled the marinating steaks from the fridge and carried them past the group huddled in the living room cooing at the baby, and stepped out onto the deck. Hot air fell like a blanket on his face and he heard Jason exclaim behind him. It was dusk and the dark trunks of oak trees shimmered slightly in a golden sunset.

"So you like it out here?" Jason said, pulling on his beer and watching Andrew transfer steaks to the massive gas grill that had been his in-laws' house-warming gift.

"Sure, it's okay."

"I guess there are some benefits to this whole home-buying thing," Jason muttered a few minutes later.

Andrew glanced up and noticed the woman he'd seen before leaning against the rail of her deck, twirling a wine glass in her hand. Her hair was pale blond, he saw in the daylight, not silver. She was dressed this time, a white fitted blouse and turquoise trousers. She turned and peered at him, lifting the glass slowly to her lips and taking a long swallow.

The grill hissed and Andrew looked down in time to save the steak from being engulfed in flames. When he looked up a minute later the woman was gone.

On Monday, Christine left for work with both boys strapped into car seats in the back of her Volvo. She would drop them off at her mother's, where they spent their days being spoiled by Nana and an elderly housekeeper named Winnie, before driving to her downtown law practice.

Usually, Andrew left for work at the same time, but this summer was different. The move had delayed the writing of a paper he had to present at a conference in late summer, and he'd set up a home office to work on it without interruption.

Except he couldn't seem to concentrate. In their apartment, his desk had been in an alcove near the front window where he'd watched city life passing by and had gotten used to the noise—sirens and delivery trucks, children laughing, neighbors bickering. It was so quiet in his new neighborhood that he jumped at the screeching of a bird in the woods behind the house. The only regular noises were the sounds of lawns being mowed by the landscape crews that arrived regularly to tend to all the larger, expensive houses. They came next door every Tuesday—Henry called it the castle house because it was a large stone Tudor with a turret. Andrew thought of it as the naked yoga house, but he'd never told Christine. Every morning he saw the man zoom away in a silver Porsche, but he had not seen the woman again.

That afternoon, fed up with his inability to produce anything coherent, he decided to go for a run. He often used the treadmills at the university gym, but it didn't seem worth it to drive that far. There were plenty of paths throughout the vast swaths of borough parkland. He drove a quarter-mile to a small horseshoe of unpaved parking where he left his car next to others and headed off on a trail. He ran hard for two miles.

On his way back he ran into his neighbor. She was running along the path toward him, wearing a green singlet and thin black running shorts, her hair pulled back severely in a ponytail which swayed side-to-side as her legs and arms moved like pistons. On one arm she had a silver bracelet that chimed faintly as she ran.

She was a faster runner and focused. She stared straight ahead and Andrew thought she would pass without speaking. He spoke instead. "Hello."

"Hi." She barely glanced at him.

Already she'd moved two paces past him. Afterward, when he dreamed of her, it would begin with this moment when he could have let her go, pretended he didn't know her. He turned and called out, "I think we're neighbors. I'm Andrew Durbin."

158 // Pittsburgh Noir

She looked back and surveyed him, standing in the path with her hands on her hips, panting. Her expression wasn't promising. After a moment she replied, "I'm Elsa." Then she said, surprising him, "Do you want to run together?"

He felt a jolt of pleasure in having been invited, like he was back in middle school and the popular girl had asked him to dance. He tried to play it cool, glancing at his watch as if time somehow factored into his decision though Christine wouldn't be home for hours. "Sure."

He had to work to keep up with her; he could feel his chest heaving, hear his labored breaths. Her own breathing seemed effortless. She ran like the deer he'd seen from the back window of his house, thin-legged and nimble, darting fluidly around trees and missing stray branches that seemed to reach out and whack him in the face.

When the path narrowed, he followed blindly, feeling damp spreading at the neck and under the arms of his T-shirt. Finally, they were back at their cars. He leaned against the hood of his Honda, sucking air, while she walked calmly over to her car, a sleek black BMW, raising a key tag to open it with a little beep. She slid into the seat and turned over the engine before poking her head out to ask, "You want to meet again on Wednesday? How about one-thirty?"

That was how it started, but he couldn't say it was ever innocent. When he got home he went straight to the shower and, leaning against the tiled wall, masturbated like a teenager, while imagining peeling the clothes off her sweating body.

She didn't talk while they ran, it wasn't her style, but she did linger sometimes afterward, once offering him some water when he'd forgotten his, and another time telling him that his stride was improving. Never once did she ask him about his life and she didn't volunteer anything. He wanted to ask about the man he'd seen on the deck, the man he assumed was her husband, judging by the thin gold-and-diamond ring set on her left hand, but he always chickened out.

Instead, he searched his garage for the free weights he'd bought at a yard sale years earlier, which had been gathering dust ever since. "What are you doing?" Christine asked when he hauled them up to their bedroom.

"Just getting back into shape."

She wrinkled her brow. "Are you trying to drop a hint?"

He looked at her standing there in a spit up–stained blouse with a dish towel slung over one shoulder. She'd taken off her jacket, but was still wearing her suit skirt, her stomach bulging over the waistline. She frowned, her round face puffy and sweaty. "Well? Because I don't appreciate the pressure."

"No, it's not for you. It's for me." He wanted to add, *You could use them too*, but he didn't.

They'd been running together for three weeks when Elsa said, "Do you want to come over for a drink?"

He'd fantasized about this moment many times, but strived to sound casual. "Why not?"

He followed her back up the hill to their quiet street, struggling to maintain the same speed, while looking out for cops, because she went seventy the whole way, the Beemer flashing along narrow roads, hardly slowing for dangerous curves.

He pulled into his own driveway and stopped outside the car for a moment, wondering if he should shower first.

"Aren't you coming?" she called, and he immediately walked across the wide expanse of emerald lawn that divided their properties.

The house was cool inside, dark after the sunshine. "This is nice," he said, admiring the midcentury modern furniture, the entire living room done in shades of black, white, and steel. She'd vanished into another room, returned with two tall glasses of ice water.

"Do you think so?" She handed a glass to him and drank her own in one long, soundless swallow, wiping the back of a delicate hand across her mouth when she finished.

"How long have you lived here?"

She smiled. "Long enough." She was standing close enough that he could see her perfectly manicured nails.

He tried to look into her eyes, but his gaze was drawn down to the erect nipples poking out of her shirt.

"Do you want to kiss me?" she said, surprising him. He felt hotter, suddenly, his vision blurred for a moment.

"I'm married."

She laughed and put her glass down on a side table, advancing toward him. "So am I."

Afterward he would think about the improbability of it, but at that moment all he thought about was the taste of her mouth and the smell and feel of her skin. It had been a long time since he'd taken time with sex, since he'd had to tell himself to slow down, enjoy it, since he'd been young enough to come immediately instead of waiting, and knowing to wait for his partner.

She didn't talk during sex either, but she made a soft little humming sound in her throat, and at the end, when they were finished, she sighed in a pleased way.

It became a pattern. They ran together three days a week, and after running they went back to her house and fucked. Once they did it in her car. Once he caught her in the woods and had her up against a tree.

He had never been this adventurous before. The closest he'd come was a night at the beach when he'd slipped his hand down Christine's blouse and would have taken her on the dunes except they heard people coming and she'd pulled away. Elsa never pulled away. She tried different sexual positions the way other women tried new shoes. The only constant was the light, rhythmic tinkling of the dozens of tiny silver bells on her bracelet.

During the rest of the week he saw her only from afar, wearing revealing dresses and three-inch sandals as she accompanied her husband in the evenings, or hiding behind enormous sunglasses while zipping off to lunch with friends. A bevy of service people came and went from the house—cleaning women, landscapers, carpenters, and pool boys. He knew she spent half her day at a spa.

One afternoon as they were loading the kids in the car to go celebrate their grandfather's birthday, Christine said, "She's well maintained," and he looked up to see Elsa, wearing a filmy white dress and gold sandals, slipping into the Porsche. She glanced over at him and away as if he were of no consequence.

The next day when he fucked her, he took her harder because of it, and when it was over he said, "Don't ignore me." She laughed.

He didn't think of sex with Elsa as making love. He didn't know her well enough to love her, but he did lust after her. He thought about her constantly, and on the days they didn't meet he found himself trying to catch glimpses of her. Once he went so far as to walk over to her house and ring the bell. He knew she was home, the BMW was there in the drive, but she didn't answer the door.

Sometimes she'd talk to him while they recovered in the cavernous bed in the dark master bedroom. He learned about her husband, that he worked in finance, that she'd met him when she was modeling, and found out that she had a German mother and American father.

In her bathroom cabinet were rows of pills, including antidepressants with her name on the bottle. She didn't appear to have a job or do any meaningful work. He asked her once and she laughed and told him her purpose in life was to look good.

Christine commented on his running so much and he talked about how good it was for him, but when she suggested that they go together in the evenings, he said he preferred to run during the day.

One afternoon, as Andrew pushed his lawn mower around the yard, Elsa's husband hailed him, coming out of the castle house wearing suit pants and a dress shirt even though it was a Saturday. "Hey there, neighbor," he said with an affable wave. He stepped gingerly across the freshly mown grass in Italian loafers. "Should have come over earlier and introduced myself. Michael Cantata." He shook hands, hard, but as Andrew released his grip, the other man's hold tightened. "I think you've met my wife," he added, looking straight into Andrew's eyes with a cold little smile.

"Yes." Andrew met his gaze for a moment, trying to keep his own eyes locked with the gray, predatory ones.

"You trim your own lawn?"

"Yeah."

"Important to take care of your own lawn. Never want to leave that unattended." He gave Andrew's hand one more squeeze and released.

"Does your husband know about us?" he asked the next day when he met Elsa in the woods. She was leaning against an oak tree doing her stretches and seemed annoyed that he'd interrupted her concentration.

"How could he know? He's at work more than ten hours a day."

He didn't believe her. Nobody could be that clueless, but maybe they had an open marriage. Christine now suspected. He caught her checking the pockets of his clothes in the laundry room. "What are you doing?"

"Are you having an affair?"

"What? No! Of course not." He'd never thought he was particularly good at lying and she stared at him for a long moment, the tension broken when Henry began crying in the other room.

"I've been going to the gym," she said the next morning, barely looking at him, already engrossed in her BlackBerry, so he thought for a moment that she was speaking to someone on the phone. When she glanced up, he realized it was meant for him.

"Great. That's great."

"I've lost five pounds."

"Wow! Good for you." He patted her shoulder as he got up from the kitchen table.

The next time they fucked he told Elsa that they had to end it. She laughed and he realized his timing had been bad, that it would have been believable if he'd said it before having sex instead of after.

He told himself every afternoon that this would be the last time, but promptly forgot his resolve the minute he saw her. He'd known a few addicts—the colleague who really had three-martini lunches and secreted a bottle of scotch in her desk drawer, a former neighbor's glassy-eyed teenage son who'd been sent to rehab for cocaine addiction, Christine's roommate from college who threw up in the bathroom after every meal—and he'd pitied them all, never understanding what it meant to have desire consume you like a rash.

One day he found a bruise on Elsa's arm. He knew her

body intimately by then and the spreading purple flower jumped out at him. "How did you get this?"

She moved out of his grasp and he saw, then, that the petals of the flower corresponded to fingers larger than his. "He grabbed you here? Is he hurting you?"

He flashed to a man's fist wrapped in silver hair at three o'clock in the morning, though he'd never told Elsa about the first time he'd seen her.

"He's not a happy man," she said. "He's not happy if anyone else is happy."

He fantasized about leaving Christine and marrying Elsa, but these thoughts lasted about as long as his orgasm. She was a kept woman, a trophy wife, and she wouldn't leave the man who provided for her. And his role in this charade was to be the plaything. He told himself it was a summer fling and it would end before the new semester started.

They were past the two-month mark when Henry came down with a bad chest cold. "We can't possibly drop him off with my mother," Christine said. "She's old and Winnie's downright elderly." She glanced at her BlackBerry, then at him. "I've got depositions all morning and then I've got to be at a hearing in the afternoon, but I can probably take off a little early. Five-thirty maybe? So you can take care of him until then, right?"

He watched over his son, took Henry's temperature, snuggled with him in the family room while they stared at *Sesame Street* on the flat screen, and plied him with apple juice, all the while thinking about Elsa waiting for him in the woods. It started to drizzle in the afternoon and he thought of Elsa out in the rain, of her standing on the pathway in a sopping wet T-shirt, of taking her there, under the boughs of a hemlock tree. He left Henry sleeping fitfully and masturbated in the shower.

Three days later Henry's fever broke, and the next morning he went back to his grandmother's house. Andrew counted the minutes until he could meet Elsa, driving fast but carefully down hillside roads slick from rain.

Her car was there, but she wasn't. He walked around it, looking for a note, and pressed his face against the tinted glass to try and see inside, but there was no evidence that she'd thought about him.

Disappointment left him sour and restless. He ran anyway, following their same trail, though it was masochistic in the pouring rain, his legs sprayed with mud, his feet slipping over wet tree roots. He thought he could catch her if he ran faster and pushed his body. When he came to the fork in the trail and had to choose, he thought he saw her imprint in the mud and took the path to the right, which got progressively steeper.

Along a narrow ridge high above the creek he tripped over a rock and fell, scraping his right shin and landing heavily on a knee. He was lucky he didn't slip over the side, skittering down the hillside with the pebbles he'd kicked loose. He pushed himself up, glancing down at the swollen creek rushing fast some twenty feet below. Among the green and brown, he noticed something pink in the water. He leaned forward, bracing his body against a maple sapling, blinking the water out of his eyes, but he couldn't tell what it was.

He ran more slowly down the hill, trying to keep the thing in view as he drew closer, ignoring the stinging scrape on his leg and the pain in his knee. When he came to the bank of the creek he could see something resting under the water.

He undid his shoes and slid off the bank, the water frigid despite the heat of the day, his toes sinking in muck, a swirl of silt disturbing his view. He reached forward blindly, stirred his arm in the soup, and felt rocks and leaves and something harder, heavy, which had settled at the bottom. He tugged and it burst out of the water, spraying him in the face, a woman's running shoe, white stained brown by the water with pink stripes and pink laces. It was Elsa's.

For a moment he did nothing but stand there, staring at the dripping shoe dangling from his hand. Then he looked wildly around . . . expecting what? To see someone in the trees watching him? The rain fell in a steady curtain, but he plunged down the creek anyway, blindly searching, his hair sopping and stringy in his eyes, his feet long since numb.

He could feel his heart thudding in time with the rushing water. He didn't think about the shoe in his hand, didn't think about the slender foot it belonged to, didn't think about what he was really looking for in the creek. Until suddenly he spotted her, lodged in the crux of an oak tree's roots, which had spread from the eroding bank like fingers raking the water and acted like a sieve, capturing anything solid that came within reach. She was facedown, her head pinned by the tree, arms forward as if she were going for a swim, except one arm was at an odd angle, as if it had been twisted, and her long, bare, muscled legs bobbed uselessly behind her, the other shoe still on its foot.

He fought the current to get to her, sobbing at the sight of her pale, perfect skin and hair laced with flotsam—broken bits of fern, splinters of bark, the single teal claw of a crayfish. He grasped her shoulder, turning her over, and saw a large, gaping wound on one side of her head, a hole really, the hair near it matted and bloody. He thought he caught a glimpse of gray matter underneath that, before he let her flop facedown again in the water.

She was dead. The closest he'd come to a dead person had

been a nine-year-old's view of his grandmother lying heavily powdered and stiff in a shiny box, but he knew Elsa was gone even before he'd seen her eyes clouded over like a dead trout. He pictured her husband waiting along the trail and striking her with a tire iron as she turned the corner.

With shaking hands he pulled his cell phone free of his wet pocket to call 911 but stopped short, suddenly realizing that he had bigger things to fear than Elsa's body floating in the water.

If he told the police about Michael Cantata's violence they would ask how he knew and he would have to confess to the affair. And Christine would kill him if she found out about it. Divorce him at the very least. If he survived her wrath he faced a future in which he only got to visit Henry and Sam every other weekend and had to share the title of "Dad" with another man. He knew Christine wouldn't live alone. She'd find someone just to spite him and someone who made more money or who wasn't going to lose his hair or who already belonged to the stupid country club.

And this was his future only if the police believed that Michael Cantata and not Andrew had done the killing. Why should they believe him? He was the one standing in the water with the body.

Panicked, Andrew peeled off his soggy T-shirt, swiped roughly at the spot on Elsa's shoulder that he'd touched, and then backed away from the body before turning and splashing back up the creek, fighting the current to get away. It wasn't until he'd climbed out on the bank that he realized he was still holding Elsa's shoe. He wiped it down frantically before hurling it back in the center of the creek where it sank with a horrific splash before bobbing slowly to the surface. He scrambled into his own shoes, fingers fumbling with the laces, feet squelching in the soles. He walked back along the trail, watching the rain eroding his footprints in the mud, until he got to the fork; he took the left path and ran down it fast, so that if someone had seen him, he could say that he'd taken this trail and had never been near the creek.

When Andrew got back to the parking lot there were no cars except his and Elsa's. They were visible from the road. How many people had passed by and seen his car? His stomach cramped when he remembered that he'd touched the BMW, and he forced himself to walk casually over. When there were no cars whizzing by he rubbed his T-shirt across the windows to smudge any potential prints.

He didn't remember driving home. He was in the mud room ineffectively drying himself with paper towels while water puddled around him when Christine appeared in the doorway.

He jumped. "Hi!" His voice sounded manic. "I didn't expect you home so soon. Are the boys with you?"

"My mother's bringing them home in a little while. They're enjoying playing in the rain." She stared at him and he forced his gaze up to her standing there in a terry cloth robe with comb marks visible through her damp hair. "You were out running in this weather?"

He nodded, ducked his head again. "Crazy. This rain is unbelievable." He was shaking, but she didn't comment. "Could you get me a towel?"

He stayed in the shower for twenty-five minutes, hoping the noise covered his sobbing. Then he ran his clothes through the washer. Christine joined him in the laundry room and said she would do it with the regular wash, but he insisted. He moved his shoes into the laundry room too, cleaning off every bit of mud before turning them upside down on an old newspaper to dry.

All that long afternoon and evening he expected to hear sirens, but they never came. He wondered if they'd found Elsa's body yet and watched the evening news braced for an announcement, but there was nothing.

At night the magnitude of what he'd done weighed on him and he couldn't sleep. He was letting a man get away with murder. He was sure Elsa's husband had killed her. He thought of writing an anonymous letter to the police to alert them that this was no accidental death, but if he fingered Michael Cantata then that long finger would eventually touch him. They would find out about his affair, and when they found out, so would Christine.

It suddenly occurred to him that this was Michael Cantata's intent: He'd killed his wife to frame Andrew, who'd been foolish enough to think that washing away his footprints and rubbing off her car windows could erase his presence from Elsa's life. His fingerprints were all over her house.

What day did her cleaning service come? Did they clean well enough to remove all traces of him from the house? His stomach roiled. He couldn't sleep until finally he did, only to dream over and over of Elsa's body floating in the water.

They were eating breakfast at the kitchen table when he heard the faint sound of a siren. He finished chewing his bite of toast, swallowed down a dry throat. The wailing grew louder and louder. He forced himself to take a bite of eggs, but Henry pushed back from the table and ran to the living room window to see. "Henry, come back to the table," Christine called.

"There's police at the castle house!"

For one long moment nothing happened. Andrew leaned over to wipe oatmeal off Sam's face, but he could feel Christine staring at him. He wouldn't meet her gaze. She abruptly stood up and stalked out of the room.

"The police are at the Cantata's," she called, confirming what Henry had said. He got up and unhooked Sam from his highchair, swinging him onto his hip and carrying him into the living room. He watched officers at the door speaking to Michael Cantata and all the while could feel the sound of his own heartbeat. He wondered if anyone else could hear it.

"What do you suppose happened?" Christine said, and her voice sounded odd. She was holding Henry's hand tightly in her own. Then he heard a faint, familiar tinkling and saw, dangling from her wrist, a silver bracelet with tiny silver bells.

FAR BENEATH

BY CARLOS ANTONIO DELGADO

Morningside

1

Downstairs in the dining room Mami looks at the table, at the big white poster paper she put there, holding a thick black marker to make thick black lines to make our Chores Chart. It is summertime now, she says, so we all have chores: vacuum, mow, Comet, Windex. She's showing us golden stickers for when we do our chores and blank spaces for when we don't. Tomorrow, she says, we start.

Tomorrow comes. I am in the upstairs plugging in the vacuum, in the small room Papi made an office, and Mami all the way in the basement cleans the toilet and the mirror and the sink. Emilio, I don't know where he is, he's only seven, so Mami gives him fake chores like separating colors from whites into piles. I am nine, I've got the vacuum. The outlets are funny in Papi's office, small, two holes (not three), both the same size, not one side big and one side little and one on the bottom (like the ends of the plug I'm holding), so I bend down to see can they fit, will they fit, do they fit, bending down then kneeling down, all the way down, leaning and leaning. And this is when I find it: a magazine. A magazine under the bookcase. A magazine I see under the bookcase when I am leaning and leaning and leaning. The one man is wearing a dark coat and a dark hat in the first picture. The other man is wearing no clothes and he has big privates. The one man is opening his dark coat and showing you his big privates. The other man is touching and kissing the one man and licking his privates and putting his privates into his mouth and into his hands and into his butt. Mami is all the way downstairs and Emilio is I don't know where, and I am right in here, right here with it, here it is, I see it, it is a magazine.

In bed tonight I close my eyes but I see the mayonnaise-water on their faces, on their necks and cheeks and tongues. I see them holding their privates, licking, licking. I see their muscles and their movement. I see their hair brushed perfectly, their white white teeth, their wide-open mouths, their eyes that like me. I see their shining backs, and chests, and legs, and butts, their feeling good touching each other. Inside my body my stomach is flopping again and again and again like water that comes down the rocks. I get hard down there. I do not like it and I do like it. I turn onto my tummy when I am hard down there and I press my face into my bedsheet and I squeeze my pillow between my legs and I press my privates into the mattress. It feels good. I think of the men and their privates and their faces liking me and I do not like it and I do like it and it feels good to feel the mattress.

2

Papi teaches summer school Spanish at Peabody High. In the morning he is already gone. Good. I am glad.

We live in Morningside, on the part of Duffield Street where instead of black asphalt they kept red bricks as the street, like olden days. Mami loves our house, she says it all the time how much, loves the brick look of the front, loves the round-top red front door, the big window over our porch, loves the garden she keeps, loves all those flowers and vines, loves the white-flower dogwood she and Papi planted last year. She loves our neighbors across the street, Dave and Richard, Papi calls them gay-bors and everybody laughs, who plant tulips in November, and she loves the hundreds and hundreds of them in spring when they grow up in all the many colors. She loves the red bricks as the street, the feel you get when you eat cereal on the porch looking at Dave and Richard's yard, leaning back in your green chair or rocking on the porch swing, saying hello to Garrett and Molly on bicycles, and to little Luci and Luci's mother Mary-Beth while they walk Elsie the dog. It's a skinny red and dark-red brick house, it's a good house, it's a tall house, and Emilio and I share the tippy-top third story for a bedroom, a bedroom like our very own tiny house. Through the window up there I can see down over all of East Liberty and up to Highland Park, I can see down into Heth's Park where we go with the Frisbee to help Luci run Elsie, I can see all up and down Duffield Street until it turns into trees, and I can see almost all the way to Peabody where Papi works.

3

Papi who is dark. Papi who is strong. Papi who speaks to me in Spanish. Papi with black hair and wrinkled forehead and thick chest and the big meat fútbol legs. Papi who holds me, wrestles me, teaches me fútbol Saturdays at Heth's. At night when he puts me to bed he breathes on me and, kissing me, hugging me, he smells like the darkness of his skin, like the darkness of earth.

4

In the mornings after Papi leaves, only when Mami is cleaning other parts of the house far away from me, that's when I go to the magazine. I look at the faces and bodies. It makes me hard down there and my thing gets bigger. It makes my back tickle inside my skin, up to my shoulders, and down to make my bottom feel good, like I am afraid, like I am happy. My legs twitch up high, close to my thing. My face feels like liquid is filling up my cheeks. My arms are like they are falling off. Only the times when Papi is already gone to teach and Mami cleans the kitchen or windows or downstairs bathroom, then I go to Papi's office to underneath the bookcase with my fingers pulling out the magazine. And when I'm looking at the magazine the blood moves all throughout my body so so fast it makes my ears stop hearing stuff.

One night in the middle of summer I am in my bed thinking about the men. Emilio is almost falling asleep up in the tippy-top, but not me. Mami and Papi are downstairs watching TV, they have left already from putting us to bed, and I sneak over to Emilio's bed and my thing is hard and big and I say to him, whispering, No, put your hands down here, like this, like that, watch first how I do it, there, like that. I say, Kiss me here and I will kiss you there too, no, kiss by sticking out your tongue. He gives me his tongue and I give to him mine and pretty soon I feel his body twitching just like my legs that twitch, and he makes a noise like crying mixing with laughing. I tell him, Shut up. They'll come back if you do that.

5

Emilio and I are upstairs in Papi's office where I have been bringing him to see the magazine. But I don't show him where it is. No way. First, I make him stay out in the hallway because, I tell him, it's a secret, a magic spell I have to chant that makes the magazine come to us. Then I close the door and I pull out the magazine from underneath the bookcase and I look at it and I am already getting hard down there, and the feeling in my mouth is like I am ready to eat soup, my saliva is stingy under my tongue, like I am nervous and hungry-thirsty at the same time. Then I open the door and he is there, saying, Where is it, let me see it, can I hold it, but I tell him, Shut up or I will make it go away, and then we are kneeling on the floor never talking, and I am turning and turning the pages.

Mami comes in to say Luci and Garrett and Molly are at the front door waiting with Elsie the dog. Have we finished our chores? Do we want to go to Heth's, to run Elsie with the Frisbee? But before I can do anything about it, she sees the magazine. I look behind me and there she is talking about Garrett and Molly and Luci and Elsie, and my butt freezes in place. She is wearing her gloves and a hat for the garden. Her shirt is light blue and wet on her tummy and sides because her body is sweaty. Her face stops talking and stops moving and then her whole entire body stops too, and I want to cry, but I hold my breath.

She does not say words. She does not even look mad. She comes over to the magazine. She picks it up, she looks at it, she closes the pages. Her face and her body do not tell me anything. She walks into her bedroom and, when she gets in there, she closes the door. I am still holding my breath, and Emilio is saying her name into his shirt sleeve, Mami, Mami, Mami, the same sound again and again, but here we are alone in Papi's office and Luci and Garrett and Molly wait downstairs, yelling, Sergio! Emilio! Are you coming or what?

6

Some nights I do not go over to him in his bed—some nights I do not even think about it. But other nights, tonight, the men are in my brain, the way they like me, their tongues, their teeth, the way their faces say, I like you, you make my body change, I want to change your body, and my butt gets tickly down through my legs and I press my privates into the mattress. In a little while when Emilio is asleep I go into his bed and he wakes up and we take off our pajamas and rub our things in the quiet dark, alone not crying, liking it and not liking it, his fingers and my fingers moving everywhere until I-don't-know-what makes my whole body, makes everything, everything like heartbeats coming out my eyeballs.

What is this? I do not ask out loud. I ask only in my stomach.

7

Heth's Park is cut out of the woods, a field that doubles for baseball and fútbol, with a playground and tennis courts on one side and the leftover woods on the other, woods that come right up to the grass field, those trees that lead to nowhere. In the morning, in the late morning that turns into lunchtime, Saturday morning, fútbol morning, Papi cleared his throat, probably he wanted to tell us something, but he did not look at us, and he did not say words. I slipped on my shin guards and my cleats (everybody so quiet, everybody moving slowly), and once more Papi cleared his throat, that rumble.

Papi and Mami—all morning this morning, all night last night—have been fighting, the long loud yells in their bedroom, the bad words, Puto! Maricón! and wet loud fat tongue throat saliva sounds, plus the long (very long) nothing-silence Papi made (after yells and cries, after screams and cries), nothing-silence comes from his face, nothing-silence sucks you in, nothing-silence makes you feel slippery and heavy and hot and want to go away, makes you afraid, nothing-silence pulls your stomach. Then, Bitch! Motherfucker! Cabrón! Joto! all night. In the morning, when Papi went to shower, Mami muttered something, muttered, Do you want your own cock? The nothing-silence Papi gave was long and horrible, his eyes locked, his forehead never moved, and Mami went on screaming again after that.

After he was dressed, Papi said to Emilio and me, To Heth's! and we—los tres, the three, the men, the guys, los caballeros—walked to Heth's. (The only Mexicans in Pittsburgh, Papi has said before. Can't find a good burrito anywhere. What is ground beef doing in my enchilada? he has joked, shaking his head.) Here were we, the men, the cholos of Morningside, the Mexico of Morningside, of Pittsburgh, Papi carrying the yellow-and-blue ball and bright green cones, and I held all the cleats, and Emilio (little, brown, skinny, quiet) held the shin guards in a bundle to his chest. We moved down the red brick street to the place where Duffield meets Morningside Avenue and hooked left onto it. At the stop sign we turned right onto Hampton, and we walked down the little hill to Heth's. Papi's fútbol legs came down dark brown and strong, the muscles moving, lifting, sinking, lifting, as he walked. Emilio was in front, his small and round head, his hair that flopped when he stepped. And all around me was Pittsburgh, the skinny crooked streets of Morningside, the green fat trees on hills, and I felt that hot heavy wet heat of summer on my neck. And we, the three, los caballeros, moved down the hill to play fútbol. Papi cleared his throat again, his throat like wet cement, and in a minute he did it again. He looked up and he looked down. He said no words. That nothing-silence made me afraid.

I was tying my shoes and so was Emilio, and Papi cleared his throat again, looking at me, trying to say (no, I mean *actually* saying), Your mami, saying, She said you found—

8

I stopped tying my shoes. My body was a rock. A statue. A

mountain. I held my breath. I pinched Emilio, who was sitting next to me. Pinched him to keep him quiet. Pinched him on the back where Papi could not see. With fingernails I pinched him, not with fingertips. Emilio jerked, barely, and he kept his mouth shut up. Papi tried again to say stuff, and I made my fingernails sink into Emilio, into his skin, and he stayed still, feeling it. Papi saying, Under the bookcase, where— And then Papi saying nothing. For a long time there was no sound and inside my body I felt everything move, like I wanted to poop, like I was up a tree in hide-and-seek, it was a *something*, a thing I cannot speak the name of, a what is it, a feeling like hunger, and like worry, and like joy, all these come together lifting me, plus the desire to weep and be covered, a cold heavy white smoke that moved through my stomach and arms and feet and face. Papi closed his eyes. Mierda! he said. Shit! Tie your shoes. Give me the ball.

9

Emilio and I in the tippy-top, night darkness up in here, our hiding place, the window open letting in soft wind, my fingers were touching and moving his thing. He licked me down there when I told him to, and I licked him down there and held him in my mouth. He lay sprawled on his bed while we were doing this—*we were doing this, we were doing this*—his eyes open, then closed, then open, now looking at the ceiling, now looking down at me, his mouth shut as he breathed through his nose. He stretched his legs, his feet, his toes, he stretched his arms and fingers, he stretched and stretched and every part of his body was tight, he moved his thing in my mouth while I licked, and licked, and licked, and I licked him until his body came loose again.

10

Fourth of July in the morning, Emilio and I were down the basement stairs, so quiet, saying lowly, No, don't touch that step, it's the loud one, while Mami and Papi stayed upstairs fighting, screams and nothing-silence, bad words and crying. Down in the garage, we were on our bikes, out the garage door, shutting it so no one heard. Get out before they hear us, I was thinking. We rode down Duffield to Garrett and Molly's house, but no one was home. We rode to Luci's. No one there either. Fourth of July means no one stays home. So in a little while we were at Heth's, and we met the man Tony in the white T-shirt who had his dog and Frisbee, running the dog everywhere just like we did with Elsie sometimes.

11

Tony, in a white T-shirt, gray sweat shorts, white socks, yellow shoes, with hairy legs and arms and white skin and long brown hair, came over to us with his Frisbee. Tony said, Hi, I'm Tony. Happy Fourth! Tony said, Would you like to help me run Lewis? That's Lewis, my dog. And Tony gave me the blue Frisbee and let me and Emilio throw it. Once, Lewis ran after it and then ran not back to us but under a tree at the edge of the field, and Tony laughed and said, Darn dog, he doesn't always bring it back.

Tony said, I like your bikes, and Tony said, Look how far I can throw it! and he threw the Frisbee all the way across the fútbol field. Tony said, Are you coming back tonight, for the fireworks? We told him Mami and Papi said we were, but we didn't know now. Tony asked Emilio and me, Do you think you can run as fast as Lewis? We called Lewis over and Tony said, Go! and Emilio and Lewis and I ran all the way across the field, and Lewis won.

Tony said, Let's send Lewis on a hunt, and Tony threw the Frisbee into the little woods, those trees, those trees, and Tony said, Lewis! Lewis! Go get it, boy! But Lewis didn't go. Go ahead, Lewis! Go on, boy! But Lewis didn't move. Tony asked would we want to help him look for the Frisbee. I asked, What about poison ivy? Tony laughed and said, I'll carry you if we see any. Let's go!

12

The small woods behind Heth's Park crowded around us, and, looking up through the trees, you saw the white and blue and yellow, the shapes and colors of daylight, and you saw the green tops of trees in the wind like fingers that close together. All kinds of sounds, small noises, our shoes on the ground, crunch, crunch, Lewis sniffing around, birds moving, squirrels crawling, and, far far off, people's voices in their backyards and driveways, came to my ears. Lewis went off to sniff stuff while Tony showed us his privates, touching his thing, making it bigger, it moving up, up, up, big like the men in the magazine, except hairy, and smelly. He said to touch it, and I did, he said to tickle it, and I did, he told Emilio and me to kiss it, and we did. He leaned against a tree and Emilio and I kept kissing his thing, and he said, Now lick it, and we did.

Even though I did not want to, I got hard down there. Tony said, Open your mouth, wider, use your tongue, and I liked it and I did not like it. Tony said, I'm going to—and he didn't finish his words. And he said, You are—and he stopped saying stuff again. My eyes were open, my hands were touching his thing, my breath puffed out between licks, my thing was very hard, and my stomach, burning, afraid, happy, became a wide heavy stone no one can find, buried far beneath the earth.

13

But in the nighttime, Papi, Mami, Emilio, and I have gathered the quilt, three or four pillows, and a basket with snacks, Papi and Mami quiet, standing next to one another, and we've met everyone in front of our house, Garrett and Molly and their parents, Luci and Mary-Beth and Elsie, everybody holding their own blankets and pillows and snacks, everyone saying, Happy Fourth! and we walk to Heth's to watch fireworks, loud and bright and big when they come, filling up the dark, *boom! boom! boom! boom!* Heth's has filled with people, has filled with their blankets and chairs, their flashlights and laughter, their sounds and movements of all kinds, these people everywhere on the field, women, men, kids, everywhere everyone's eyes looking up—you can see them when the lights of the fireworks flash. Far away on the other side of the field I see Tony and Lewis, Tony looking up too, Lewis sitting next to him, afraid of the *boom! boom!* Tony is wearing the same white T-shirt but now red shorts instead of gray—he does not see me watching him. I point to him, showing Emilio.

In the tippy-top tonight, when we are in our own beds, we hear the sounds of more fireworks all across Pittsburgh, hear kids run and yell, hear them chase and tell jokes, hear *boom! boom! boom!* I hear the TV downstairs and I hear Mami and Papi talking loudly, not screaming. My eyes have stayed open a long time and I see Tony in my brain, see him take off his shorts, see the hair on his legs like a thousand black wires, see the way he smiles and says, Come on, I'll show you, and I see those men from the magazine, and Emilio, and—what do I know? I know I do not want to say, I like it. I know it feels strange and scary to say, I want more. And I know I am afraid when I am feeling happy. What do I know? I know about the darkness, and I like the darkness, like how it surrounds me. I know I like to make bodies change, like how the men make my body change, like how I move next to Emilio to make his body like my body, softly in the dark, at first feeling shy, and after a long time still we do not say words, just breathe, and fear, and touch. My stomach rises, falls, will rise again, and my thighs will burn, and everywhere my body will fill, fill up, and—what, what next, what comes next? I will cover him and desire him and seek to touch him everywhere.

PART IV

Neighbors Who Care

AT THE BUENA VISTA

BY HILARY MASTERS

Mexican War Streets

A t the Buena Vista, we had almost what you might call a private club, what with Malcolm keeping an eye out through the front window blinds for people off the street, black people and such who didn't quite fit. They wouldn't be happy in the place.

"Here comes one," Malcolm might say. "Quick, lock the door."

And Jerry Warner would put down his Rolling Rock and turn the latch on the front door and we'd just sit quiet, only the phony laughter on the TV show going on, as we listened to the footsteps outside pass by. They never once hesitated and we could hear them while they just kept walking, as I guess Malcolm's attitude was well known in the neighborhood, and we didn't about it much.

Jerry always took the stool next to the door so that if his coughing got the best of him he could whip outside in a hurry to right himself and not disturb the rest of us. The VA told him his lungs were a fucking wonder considering the shit he got into in 'Nam, but he would have his moments hacking like he might be coming apart. And he was always so apologetic, how could you be annoyed with him, and besides, anybody complaining would have to answer to one or two of us who were also vets of that war.

But that wouldn't be the case anyways, for like I said, it

was a cozy place and we had everything right there that we needed. Within reach. The cooler packed with beer; Malcolm would also put in some I.C. Light so as to offer a choice, and the different chips in their bright packages in front of the mirror gave off a warmth. Whoever ate any of the pickled eggs was a mystery to me, for there always seemed to be the same four of them resting in their juice at the bottom of the jar. Sometimes when Malcolm opened the cooler to serve one of us, all those cans of beer neatly racked reminded me of shells waiting to be loaded into a battery's magazines. And he had a microwave to heat up the packages of dehydrated soup he'd mix up with water on order. Chicken noodle was the favorite and so we wanted for very little.

It was also a kind of haven for some of us who hadn't quite learned how to get used to the neighborhood as new people began to fix up some of the old houses, sometimes ripping out the whole inners and putting in real fancy fittings, and repainting the fronts, new stones in the stoops—and I had a hand in some of them. You could hardly recognize a street and almost get lost going home from the Buena Vista, like the houses might have grew different while you were sipping your beer inside the bar. You'd meet some of these new people, all young and bright eyed as they came into the bar, and Malcolm would tell them what was on hand, so they never stayed long, never came back.

But the big excitement for us was hearing Malcolm tell about his old Aunt Sally and her dog. The old lady lived in Troy Hill but kept up with the news of the neighborhood because she still had distant relatives living at the top of the street. Her family had lived there since it was known as Allegheny City, and in fact she still owned the building the bar occupied and the house next door that she rented out to a welfare family. That always graveled Malcolm, he'd go on for a good hour about how the house next door was going practically rent free to that family on the roll when he could get three or four times more for it if he had any say about it. Also, he lived upstairs over the bar, and the people renting the house next door were a noisy bunch with that girl of theirs bringing men back to sit on their stoop at all hours. It was going shabby, no argument about it, and becoming an eyesore for the neighborhood.

"'Look at that dawg. That dawg is dead, Aunt Sally,'" he told us he'd say to the old lady, hoping she'd get the idea for herself. She was close to the dog, about all she cared about. He'd visit her every Sunday, but more than a social call, he'd come to check out her breathing since she was connected to some oxygen. "'Everything connected okay?' I ask her, sometimes I turn up a valve to make her eyes pop. It can't be too much longer," he'd say like he was holding his breath under water and then pour himself a shot of the Old Overholt he kept mostly for himself. None of us favored the whiskey, as one shot nearly equaled the cost of three Rocks, and then its sipping time was short.

He'd bring his aunt little gifts he'd somehow collected at the bar. One time he brought her a package of fruit jellies that was a promotion from the beer distributor, but they weren't a success as they got stuck in her dentures and her mouth almost had to be pried apart. That was a good laugh. "Some sight, I tell you," Malcolm said, adding fuel to our amusement. He figured he was her closest relative, and she had no one to leave her properties to, so why not him? So he'd get cleaned up on Sundays, maybe grab a package of peanuts from behind the bar, and head up to Troy Hill to sit with her through the TV shows she watched. *The Christian Hour* was a favorite, followed close by a program on family antiques people brought in to have their value assessed, and Malcolm would say he'd sit through all these programs, yelling comments into her one good ear and trying to avoid the dog. The nuts got stuck in her teeth.

The dog's name was Mitzi and she looked like a mop head that might have swept up all the floors of the Salvation Army. And it was clear she didn't like Malcolm, and had even peed on his shoes one Sunday during the *The Christian Hour*. He couldn't understand the relationship between her and Aunt Sally; he'd tell us how she would hug the little animal, even give her a whiff of the oxygen now and then like it might cement the bond between them. "But I don't care," he said one afternoon good-humoredly. "A little baptism now and then is good for the soul." He put one foot up on the sink behind the bar like some high school athlete being a regular guy. "When I get down to Boca Raton in all that sunshine, I won't care if that little mongrel has taken a dump on me. I'm going to leave all you bums behind."

So Malcolm had his plans for after Aunt Sally passed on. He'd sell the bar and throw the welfare people out and sell that house too. It was hard not to feel happy for him about his future; he'd get so excited about his prospects that his foot on the sink would start jiggling, and once or twice he even forgot to ring up a brew.

But when would this good fortune take place? Every Sunday he'd greet her and she'd be all rigged up with her various tubes and the oxygen pumping into her like she was a ten wheeler going west. Mitzi would be scampering about, raising up the dust, a creature gone mad with her own prospects, and the programs would be blaring on the TV. Well, it was no place for a sane man, Malcolm said, and a test of his endurance. Some of us sympathized with him and all enjoyed the scene as he rendered it. Then it was suddenly over.

The report in the *Post-Gazette* mentioned the oxygen and that a spark of some kind had set off the explosion. There was speculation that Mitzi might have loosened a connection in her play with Aunt Sally, and Malcolm in his report to the investigators mentioned that the dog had been especially active during his visit that Sunday, running up and down and all over her owner like she was a garden ornament. He said he must have got out of the house just in time, because he had been on the front steps as it blew, one window in her bedroom went completely out, and when he ran back in, there was nothing he could do. He did pull Mitzi out from beneath the bed. "I won't try to describe what I saw," he told us. "It's a sight I'll never forget." He shook his head and looked at the Pirates calendar taped on the mirror.

So there was a lot of talk and investigations, one special note in the *P-G* of how Malcolm had saved the dog. He had taken her over as her lone survivor and was something of a hero. The police asked him a lot of questions and even questioned some of us—especially Jerry. Apparently someone had told them that Malcolm had talked to Jerry a lot about the blast in 'Nam that had crippled his lungs. Of course, all of us knew about that—Jerry talked about it often, sometimes to a fault. Meanwhile, Mitzi took up residence at the Buena Vista, and she was a cute little thing the way she went up on her hind legs to greet you when you came into the bar, pawing the air, her tiny eyes bright inside all that fluffy fur. It was as if she had always belonged in the bar, belonged to us. Meanwhile, Malcolm was busy consulting with lawyers about Aunt Sally's estate—he'd give us full reports. He must have spent much of the fall downtown. And the cops kept coming around too, until finally they just quit, and Malcolm signed a lot of papers. "Here's the ticket to Boca Raton," he told us one afternoon, holding up a bunch of legal papers that he asked me to witness, which I did gladly. I didn't read them, that sort of mumbo-jumbo is not in my line, and he set up a round for us to celebrate.

Then a whole set of new lawyers and officials began to show up, looking at the bar, taking measurements, and talking to the family next door. It turns out that Aunt Sally had left the whole kit and caboodle to that television program, *The Christian Hour*. They kicked out the welfare family next door and put the house up for sale. It was snapped up quick by a couple that looked like people off a cereal box—and with a child of about two. And they in turn hired lawyers to start the works turning to close down the place, saying the Buena Vista was a "public nuisance." All of which came as news to us because we weren't loud or disorderly and most of us were vets. All through it, Malcolm kept up his spirits like a guy on a sinking ship, but I guess the final blow came when this bunch of people walked in one afternoon and started measuring the bar and the back of the place where they planned to put a kitchen. All of us were told to find a new place to go, including Malcolm who had to pack up his things as well.

I kept Mitzi, and the two of us make pretty good company for each other.

HOMECOMING

BY KATHRYN MILLER HAINES

Wilkinsburg

H e stepped onto the platform at the Pennsylvania Railroad Station and heard the Veterans of Foreign Wars Band strike up the national anthem. Mothers and fathers, children and wives had come out to see the returning soldiers. He scanned the crowd for Lorraine, but the mass of humanity crowding the platform did not include her. He felt his spirits sink. He'd tried to persuade himself she would come.

As soldier after soldier passed through the station and onto Hay Street, the sounds of the band were broken up by a new cacophony: honking horns, ringing church bells, whistles from the mills and locomotives. There was joy all around him.

My God, how women had changed—the shorter skirts, the bare, smooth legs, what seemed to him garish makeup, and then the confidence with which they took over the streets. She was changed now too. He knew it from her letters.

And her not being here—

Still, in spite of what he knew, he waited. He hung back near the entrance of the station, trying to avoid the flood of people that wanted to push him across Hay Street toward the new municipal building. The humidity was overwhelming— already his dress uniform felt damp. The clock above the train station crept toward the half hour. From his vantage he could see the trolley cars as they followed the yellow line up and down Penn Avenue. They paused and unloaded their passengers. No Lorraine.

After an hour's wait, he started up Ross Street, following the familiar path home. He passed the post office, Buke's Grill, and the Ross Avenue Methodist Church, where he was baptized and married. He passed beneath the shadow of the Carl Building where people streamed in and out, on their way to and from doctor's appointments. His heart pounded. He tried to ready himself for the confrontation.

Oaks lined the road, shielding the Queen Anne and Romanesque houses from the harsh summer sun, houses similar to the one he was now headed toward. They had bought it a few months before he was called up, thinking it the perfect place to raise a family. Plans—oh, they'd made them. He was supposed to land a job at Westinghouse, just like his father had. They'd buy a brand-new car at Bauman Chevrolet. He would join the Elks and volunteer to coach one of the sandlot football teams. Lorraine said she'd volunteer for their church and the Young Women's Christian Association (he was passing their building right now). They'd put their children, when they came, into scouts and the youth orchestra.

None of those plans had presupposed the war. Or men who didn't go to war.

Lorraine had cried the day the telegram arrived. She cried at everything, happy or sad, granted, but she loved him then. Or so he thought.

He didn't know anymore.

His bag was heavy. He wanted to stop, but he kept going. A couple walked in front of him, hand in hand, the guy's blue jacket casually tossed over his shoulder. The man turned slightly and offered him a polite nod before turning back to his companion. The woman was talking, talking, filling the man in on everything he'd missed and everything they'd do now that he was home safe. The man listened in silence, a curious smile on his face.

His arm ached where a bullet wound permanently puckered the skin. He paused and massaged the muscle, then wound up his shoulder like a pitcher on the mound. He'd been soft before the war; now he was lean and sinewy, his face permanently creased by things he'd seen that he wished he could erase from his mind.

The neighborhood had changed very little in four years. There were trinkets of patriotism everywhere he looked: Old Glory waving from poles, starred flags winking from windows, flowers chosen because of their hues of red, white, and blue.

He was a hero. He'd killed four enemy soldiers, maybe more. He'd found out he was tough.

A woman tending her garden looked up at him and smiled. "Welcome back," she said. He fought to remember her name. Mrs. Parker? Porter? She had a yippy little dog that got loose whenever it rained. He'd called the dog warden on her because of the urine pooled on his front porch. Now the woman was smiling. A new beginning, courtesy of the anonymity provided by the U.S. Armed Forces.

Letters—him trying to be the man of the house no matter how far away he was. *Don't forget to open up the damper on the furnace. You can't let a week pass without starting the car or the engine will choke, especially in the winter. Don't pay for a subscription if you're not going to read the paper every day. Tell the milkman to cut the order down to a pint.* He thinks now she hated those letters.

She wrote asking him to talk about himself. He didn't. He didn't know what to say about k-rations or the men he humped with who had nicknames like Bug and Hickory.

He kept walking and he felt his stomach drop when he passed Roger Cleveland's family home. She didn't have to say it in the letters. He just knew, the way you know a thing like that. They'd been best friends, Roger and him, until he was called up and Roger was declared 4-F.

He turned the corner. He was only two blocks from home. The image of his house remained crisp in his mind, everything about it, every inch of it. Lorraine wrote to him about it, things she was doing to the house and yard. She had hoed the earth on her own, turning the yard into a victory garden to help with the war. The first attempt didn't work. The seeds got washed away by torrential rain. She'd started again a week later and her efforts were rewarded with lettuce, carrots, tomatoes, and cucumbers.

He continued up the street, surprised to find that he now conquered with ease the hilly road that had once left him breathless. Some of the neighborhood had gotten shabbier— well, the men weren't there to fix things—porches cried for paint, sidewalks were choked with weeds, roofs needed new shingles to replace those blown off during a flurry of early-summer storms.

Lorraine had painted the inside of the house too, he knew. She'd shown him what she'd chosen by dabbing the V-mail with the wet brushes, turning the austere government-issue paper into stationery colored mint-green (living room) and a sunny yellow (kitchen). She did the work herself, she said. He didn't believe it. The news ate a hole in his stomach.

Don't do any more. Wait till I come home, he wrote.

In answer, she explained that staying at home, being a wife with no husband to tend to, was driving her crazy. *Do you miss me?* she asked in another letter. *I had a dream last night that you were with another woman. She was a pretty nurse you met at the officer's club.*

At first this letter confused him. Then he realized the question was really a . . . sort of warning, or maybe a permission, because she didn't want to say what was going on with her.

It wasn't pretty young nurses the men turned to, but prostitutes. And at first he didn't, then he did.

Her letters grew briefer. *Mr. Palmer lost two apple trees in last week's storm. We have a hornet's nest under the front porch eaves. Roger stopped by. He's working at U.S. Steel now. He told me to tell you hello.*

He was powerless from far away, so he played the guilt game. *You might want to mention the hornet's nest to Roger and see if he can take care of it for you. I'd hate to think of my girl getting stung.*

The next letter said nothing about the hornet's nest. She told about how she had to wait in a line that stretched two blocks if she wanted to buy butter at Kregar's. Isaly's no longer sold meat on Mondays. Toppers Newsstand was operating twenty-four hours a day now. *I'm going to get a job. All of the mills are hiring women.*

Don't, please, he wrote. *Mills are dangerous.*

For a while he didn't get a response. Then: *You're right. Of course you're right. Roger said the same thing. In fact, he says the women are paid barely a pittance, nothing compared to what the men make.*

Roger Cleveland. Friend turned enemy.

The Tinsley boy hasn't cut the grass the last two weeks. It's starting to look like our house has been abandoned. Do you think I should ask Roger if he would be willing to mow it?

As his time overseas came to a close, her letters arrived

less frequently. It was, a friend in his platoon assured him, something every man experienced as the war dragged on— the foothold they had at home had weakened. He'd been at war longer than he and Lorraine had known each other, five times as long as they'd been married. "Just divorce her," his friend said. "Don't look back."

"Or kill her," another man said, laughing.

"No. Kill *him*. Whoever took your place. Kill him." And that man was not laughing.

As he continued up the street, he spotted his house and saw the lawn was trimmed and neat. When he got closer, he saw the porch floor was swept, its varnish fresh enough to catch his reflection. The windows sparkled from a recent cleaning.

He half expected to see someone else's name on the mailbox as proof that the place was no longer his. But *Boyer* was still there, painted in his sure hand within days of moving in. And when he lifted the box's lid, the mail inside bore his name, some bills addressed to him, a postcard *from* him. The one that told her which train he'd be arriving home on.

He pulled his postcard from the box. For a moment, his heart lightened. She hadn't even seen it. Could she be out of town? Had she taken the mill shift after all?

He reached above the doorframe and found the spare key he had always kept there. He slid it into the lock and was surprised to find the once stubborn latch open with ease.

"Hello?" he called out as he stepped inside. "Lorraine?" He dropped his duffle to the floor, then dragged it behind the sofa. A reconnoiter. He walked around, looking. He felt like an intruder. The previous day's *Pittsburgh Post-Gazette* sat folded on the coffee table, the page with the radio schedule faceup. A coffee mug was there beside it, still half full of the weak chicory mix she drank to start her day. Bright red lip crème smeared the rim of the cup.

In the kitchen he felt the coffee pot. No, cold.

Through the window above the sink he glimpsed the backyard where the lawn lay freshly mown. The garden was going strong.

On the table lay the letter he'd sent announcing that he'd be stateside soon. He'd guessed at his date of return in that note and Lorraine had underlined this three times in dark pencil.

He left the kitchen and crept up the stairs, not sure what he was expecting to find. The second floor was, like the rest of the house, immaculate. The guest room bed was clad in a quilt he'd never seen before. The bathroom was pin neat, except for a razor sitting on the sink.

He knew. He'd known. But what to do about it?

A door opened downstairs. He slipped off his shoes and crept out of the room and into the hallway. From his vantage he could see Lorraine framed by the front door, the taxi that had deposited her pulling away from the curb. She carried a box of groceries and a cosmetics case she used whenever they went away on overnight trips. She shut the door with her hip and proceeded to the kitchen. His heart jumped. He loved her, he still loved her. He could hear her as she moved from room to room, setting down the box of groceries and her bag, switching on the radio, kicking off her shoes. He tiptoed down the stairs and hugged the wall of the parlor so he could better observe her. She was wearing a day dress he didn't recognize—black with white polka dots. Her hair was long. She looked . . . good.

She left the kitchen and began to head his way. He receded into the shadow provided by the highboy as she returned to the front door and stepped out onto the porch. With her back now to him, he took a chance and darted toward the kitchen. There he saw up close the food she'd lugged from Kregar's: a Lady Baltimore cake, steak, a couple potatoes.

She was coming back inside, this time with the mail in her hands. Her eyes were cast downward as she rifled past the bills and landed on his postcard. She sank to the sofa. He watched her. She did not look happy when she reached for the telephone and lifted the receiver. She asked for an exchange that he didn't recognize and waited for the operator to connect her.

He emerged from the shadows. "Hello, Lorraine," he said.

She looked up, startled. They stared at each other. Someone said something into the receiver and she replied in a rush: "I have to go. My husband's home." She replaced the receiver and stared at him still.

"I thought you'd be at the station. At least that."

"I'm sorry I wasn't there." Remembering the postcard, she raised it toward him, as though it were a letter *for* him, not from him. "I didn't see your postcard until just now. I thought . . . I thought next week."

"Yeah."

"What are you looking at?"

"You."

"I'm glad you're home." She stood and came to embrace him, but he caught her wrists in his hands and held her at arm's length.

"Don't lie to me, Lorraine."

Her smile faltered. "I'm not lying. You're hurting me."

He wanted to hurt her. He wanted to snap both of her arms in two. She tried to free herself from his grip, but he held on even tighter.

"Please, Bill." Her voice was tense with pain. "We have to talk."

"I think I know that." He shook her. "Do you think I'm stupid?"

"Bill, let me go. You're scaring me." Her eyes filled with tears.

He released her. She looked at the deep red marks he'd left and again they didn't say anything.

"I'm sorry," he whispered finally. "I don't know how to deal with this."

"It's all right." She rubbed the feeling back into her wrists.

"I didn't mean to hurt you."

"I know."

He didn't want to know after all. When she opened her arms wide, he sank into them and inhaled the scent of her new perfume. They held onto each other for a long time, maybe five minutes, just rocking.

The kitchen door opened and footsteps sounded behind him. He turned. It was Roger.

"Did he hurt you?" Roger asked.

"No, no." Though he had pulled away from her, she touched his arm still.

"Buddy, we need to have a serious talk."

"You can't do this." He stumbled toward his duffle, then stopped and eyed the fireplace poker, knowing he looked desperate, that he *was* desperate, the boy who went to war, not the soldier who had done the killing over there.

"Sometimes things change," Roger said. "We were hoping you would understand."

Bill started to cry. Once he started, the sobs grew louder and more ugly with each second. "I want to kill you," he blubbered. "I want to kill the both of you."

"It's all right," she said. "It's going to be all right."

"Get him a whiskey," Roger said. And she hurried to the cabinet to pull out a bottle of booze. "Sit down," Roger continued. "Have a seat. Let's take it easy."

He was tired of killing. He didn't think he could do it again.

"Sit."

He didn't know where to go. He sat. Roger handed him a tumbler of whiskey, saying something again about the way things change, they just change.

He had to go somewhere.

Tonight.

He didn't belong.

Roger Cleveland had come home.

CHEATER

BY AUBREY HIRSCH

Squirrel Hill

Alex's apartment looks like a hotel room after the guests have gone to check out. There are towels on the floor and dirty wine glasses scattered around. The bedspread came with the sheets, came with the curtains, came with the throw pillows on the couch. A complete set. The fireplace is fake. There is only generic art on the walls. No photographs. No real trace of a permanent personality. Maybe Alex is a different man with every girl he brings home. Or maybe there is no real Alex. Or maybe he just doesn't care to decorate. I tend to think people have more depth than they really do.

When I wake up the first time, the sun is nowhere in sight. So I think it'll be okay if I go back to sleep for a little while. But when I wake up again the sun has pounded its way through the shades, dropped to the floor, crawled across the carpet, over my clothes, up onto the bed, and into my hair.

I am already in a terrible mood when I gather my clothes. Luckily, it is a Saturday, so I'm not late for work. Alex is still asleep as I start to get dressed. After too many mornings spent searching in vain for my stockings, I stopped wearing them to pick up guys. So now it's my wedding ring I'm looking for when I realize that I've forgotten to take it off again.

I wake Alex up to tell him I'm leaving. He says okay and doesn't even roll over before he goes back to sleep. He stopped offering me cabs a long time ago.

202 // PITTSBURGH NOIR

April in Pittsburgh is schizophrenic. Sometimes it feels like December. Today, it feels like August. I try to read the *Post-Gazette* on the bus back to Squirrel Hill, but my head is brimming over with stories about last night and no one to tell them to. I'd never done it in a bar before. But when I replay the scene under my eyelids all I can see is that little band of gold on my fourth finger. My clothes feel heavy and out of place, like they've soaked up a little of Alex's apartment. Maybe I have too; I feel a little generic.

By the time I get off the bus, I have taken my mind off of the bar and focused it on how badly I need a shower. I spot Evan across the street. I don't know his real name, but he looks like an Evan. I can walk for blocks on autopilot without ever taking in the scenery, but I never miss Evan, even in a crowd. He's on his way to work and I curse myself for going back to sleep at Alex's. He has a folded copy of the paper in one hand and with the other he is idly twisting the little gold band mine is designed to match. I wonder if he notices me. For a second I almost feel a connection. I imagine that the rest of his paper's sitting on the kitchen table next to my clean coffee mug. I ignore the fact that I wake up at my own place so seldom that I don't even get a paper delivered there anymore.

When I get to my apartment, I notice that my clothes are starting to smell like me again, but my bag still reeks of stale cigar smoke and the Irish shower I took at Alex's. Figures. It's the only piece of my outfit I can't wash. I bet a real designer bag would blend seamlessly from life to life. The second I came back it would smell like vanilla-scented candles and carpet that's been vacuumed too often. Instead, my bag reminds me of the Squirrel Cage and how I had to try and clean up the mess between my thighs with cocktail napkins. They were the brown, recycled kind with the name of the bar screened onto them. The ink left little black streaks on my legs. Plus, I was sore and they were scratchy, but Alex was hissing at me to hurry up because the bartender was giving us looks. We got out of there and I tried to lighten things up a little by saying thanks and flashing him a secret smile. He ignored me until we got into his car and he asked if I was on the pill.

After my shower and a shot of Febreze to my bag, I try to meet Evan for lunch, but he doesn't show up to the Murray Avenue Grill at the usual time. Instead, he ambles in just as I am leaving. I open my lips to say something, but he walks past.

It is moments like these that ruin my fun, when Evan refuses to play along. I know he isn't really my husband. He's just someone I noticed on the street once and followed to work. And then home. Then to where he eats. And shops. I bought a ring that looked like his and inserted him into my fantasy. Because I don't have anyone to cheat on. And I love the rush. It makes me feel dangerous and exciting, and I am neither of those things without it. So I tell myself that it is worth the work I have to do in these moments. I reinvent the exchange. In my mind: I opened my lips to try and explain, but he mistook it for a smile and walked away.

I wake up on Kevin's couch at six a.m. He isn't next to me; I didn't expect him to be. I look for him in the bedroom, but he isn't there either. Even though the sun is still low enough to cling to the ceiling and not the floor, both sides of the bed are cold. I try the kitchen and the shower before I accept that he's gone and start to get myself together. My wedding ring is in my empty champagne glass and most of my clothes are still on from the night before.

We'd met at Fanattics, a sports bar, where I'd pretended to cheer for his hometown basketball team and he took me home with him. He led me away from the bedroom, saying his girl-friend would smell me on the sheets. We did it on the couch, which is plastic, treated to look like leather. I had to spread my jacket down under my bare legs and constantly rearrange myself to keep from sticking to it. It was less than comfortable, but the champagne we spilled and anything that leaked out of the condom were easy to wipe up afterward. I only felt a little unsanitary when I woke up with my mouth pressed against the pleather. The sex was good. I was drunk enough to be loud and he was drunk enough not to notice that I was leaving the "K" off of his name.

I walk around his apartment once, slowly. I tell myself I'm making sure I haven't left anything; but when I start to look around rooms I was never in, I realize I'm searching for some kind of goodbye. Or some sort of affirmation that I was close to someone the night before, even for a little while. I don't find anything.

I was drunk when we left the bar, so I have no idea which bus to take home from Kevin's building. Luckily, he bought the drinks and I have just enough money to cab home on.

The cab ride is my first chance to think about how I feel. I have come down completely from the night before, and I start to think about grade school when they taught us about drugs. My hair is crunchy from dried champagne that the couch didn't soak up and my legs feel sunburned from peel-ing them off the plastic. I can still taste Kevin's hair gel under my fingernails when I bite them. My bag smells like cham-pagne and pine tree air freshener. I am glad I cannot smell my heart. Seven a.m. is not a good time for me. Maybe I am going through some kind of withdrawal.

I try to focus on the positive. The cool thing about sleep-ing with different people is the constant string of surprises.

Kevin, for instance, started reciting the Our Father about twenty minutes in and didn't stop until he came. There will probably be a time when I find that creepy, but for now I am fascinated.

By the time I get to my apartment it's too late to catch Evan on his way to work. After an hour or so of doing nothing I start to feel transparent, like I'm bleeding into the wallpaper. So I shower and get the hell out of there. I don't realize where I'm going until I hit Shady Avenue. Then, I instinctively walk toward Evan's office building. Maybe it's because I feel guilty. Examining my motivations doesn't seem important.

Evan is outside on a cigarette break, a stubby Parliament looks ready to drop from his fingers. He stares right through me and I think, *Wallpaper.*

"Hey."

"Hello," he says.

I can't find any emotion in his voice at all. "I'll make this fast, I know you've got work to do. I was thinking maybe we could have dinner later in the week."

He looks confused and glances over his right shoulder. "I think I'm busy," he says, and gestures to his wedding band.

My hand instinctively goes to mine. I can't find anything between us at all. His eyes look dead and I take a second to wonder if I've killed this. I try as hard as I can to think of the perfect thing to say, but I've got the Our Father stuck in my head and I can't think of anything at all.

I walk back to the bus stop slowly and start to worry about my fantasy fading. I have a pretty safe cure for times like these. I buy things for Evan. Then I look at them and I can feel him in my apartment again. I stop into CVS and buy him a green toothbrush. I stop into Littles Shoes and buy him an expensive pair of boots. I stop into Orr's and buy him a new watch.

By the time I stop home to drop his things off, I feel much better. I can't wait to go to the Squirrel Cage later. I imagine I'm telling Evan I'm heading to a meeting and will be out late.

When I wake up, Mark is making breakfast. I quickly tie my hair back and throw on some lip gloss, then walk into the kitchen. I can hear the bacon frying before I can smell it.

"Smells good," I say.

"I'm sorry," he says, "I didn't make enough. I figured you'd be leaving."

"Oh," I say. "I am."

My stomach starts to hurt as I drag it away from the bacon smell. I think it's mad at me for filling it with so much alcohol. Fucking tequila sunrises; they're so pretty.

My clothes are thrown over a chair in the bedroom. There's nothing to look around for and no reason I can think of to prolong my visit. Not that I really want to, I just hate that surreal feeling I get on the way home: *Did that really happen?* My imagination's so good these days. Sometimes it's hard to tell. Luckily, Mark's apartment smells like kitty litter and my skirt probably does too.

Mark's place is small, but charming. The border on the wallpaper is matched up perfectly, which makes me think he has a girlfriend, even though he swore he doesn't. The furniture looks like college leftovers. There are desk chairs where there should be recliners, futons where there should be couches, beer cans where there should be vases. He called it his "bachelor pad" but it doesn't have foosball, so I don't think it counts.

The sex was unremarkable. Even when I thought he was making me breakfast, it didn't seem that great. Every time I got close he would pull back and prompt me to beg for it. I did a half-assed job just to get things going, but I wasn't into it. I also thought he got too sweaty. I was tempted to get up halfway through and switch on the ceiling fan, but I figured that would make it last longer, and at that point I just wanted to get to sleep.

By the time we finished, I was sober again and getting restless. He passed out right away and I stayed up for a little while. I wanted to know something about him. I didn't need his life story, or even his telephone number. Just something to make him feel like a real person. I walked around searching for the foosball table. Nothing. I checked his fridge to see if maybe he was a vegetarian. Nope. I looked through his wallet for photos, but I didn't find any. I learned his eye color from his driver's license and went back to bed.

On the way home I slip into withdrawal again. I feel sweaty and laced with doubt. I smell my skirt for evidence of last night. Kitty litter. I stop thinking about how delusional I might be and puzzle over why I never saw a cat.

The tequila makes my stomach feel like it's closing in on itself. I look through the cupboards to find something to prop it up with, but the only thing I have a taste for is bacon. I head to Pamela's, best breakfast in the 'burgh.

Evan is there with some woman I don't recognize. I watch them flirt back and forth for a bit, but I don't worry until he leans over to kiss her. Then I walk past, letting my heels click loudly, which I never do.

He doesn't look over. Neither of them follows me with their eyes. Their right hands are clasped across the table and the fingers on their left hands are looped through the handles of their coffee mugs. I can see their matching wedding bands. Hers looks more expensive than mine and she wears it under a diamond solitaire. They seem right together. I don't realize I've stopped to stare until Evan, or whatever his name is, glances over. I fake a yawn to hide the tears in my eyes, but he doesn't notice them anyway.

I storm out of the diner thinking some combination of *Maybe I'll buy him that expensive bathrobe* and *Now I've gone too far*. I hover over a sewer grate outside the restaurant and pull my ring from my finger. The skin is a little lighter underneath it and the feel of skin brushing skin there is foreign and unpleasant. I know Evan and I are over. I can't fix that. I struggle to tell myself: *He didn't treat me right. I'm filing for divorce.* But I know I won't feel like my dangerous, exciting self again until I'm remarried, for better or worse, for real or . . . not. I palm my wedding ring, and carefully tuck it into my purse on the ride home.

The next weekend I need an adventure, so I go to Silky's. It's mostly Pitt students watching the Penguins game, so wouldn't usually be my pick, but it's ladies' night and my drinks are free. On the way in I get a plastic cup and a black stamp on the back of each hand. I say a silent prayer that they'll fade by Monday. I take a look at my options. Too young, too short, too skinny, not in a million years, out of my league, maybe if I was drunk enough, and then I see him: perfect. He's too old to be here, at least forty, and when I glance over, a sorority girl is giving him a dirty look and storming off. I know he's not having any luck and think maybe he's as desperate as I am to get laid. I make eye contact from across the bar and sit down next to him, our legs touching. He offers me a drink and I display my ladies' night stamps. He smiles.

He asks if I'm married.

I tell him, "We're working on a divorce."

Pittsburgh scores on the television over his right shoulder.

He is drinking Guinness, so I am too, but I have a hard time getting it down. I look around at the few college girls with their pastel drinks in plastic cups.

He tells me he was married once.

"Didn't like it?"

He shakes his head.

The Guinness is starting to settle in my stomach and flutter to my brain.

He tells me his name is Rick.

"Pleasure to meet you," I say, drawing out the L so he'll think about my tongue.

The music from the juke box is so loud I can't feel my heartbeat over the bass line.

He tells me I have beautiful eyes.

"Rick," I ask, leaning in a little, "are you hitting on me?"

The barstools are too high and my feet are dangling a couple of inches above the floor. It makes me feel silly and I'm anxious to get out of here, but he orders us another round.

He asks what we should drink to.

I raise my plastic cup: "Marriage."

And we drink.

Two hours, three pints of Guinness, sixteen jam band songs, a short uphill walk, and two flights of stairs later, he's fumbling with the keys to his place and I'm squeezing his ass through his work pants. I hear the lock click and help him turn the doorknob. As soon as we get inside, he backs me up against the wall and slips his hand between my legs. The faded blue color of the room reminds me of the backgrounds on Saturday-morning cartoon shows. In my head, the Looney Tunes theme song is the soundtrack to the rest of the evening.

When I wake up, Rick is walking out the door. I dress quickly and follow him from a safe distance. I don't know where we're walking to, but on the way there I slip on my ring and start to think about our wedding. At first I can't decide where we had it, or how many bridesmaids there were. But the more I think about it, the clearer it becomes in my mind: Rick's spontaneous wide-eyed proposal, our rehearsal dinner on Mount Washington, how mad I was when he dropped his wedding ring in the drain and lost it, how he'd never suspect any infidelity on my part, how we're so in love.

This is my second husband, Rick. The green toothbrush in my bathroom is Rick's. I like the sound of it already. Rick steps into a dry cleaner's on Forbes. When thirty minutes go by and he still hasn't emerged with a couple of shrink-wrapped shirts or an off-season jacket, I copy the address into my date book, labeling it, *Rick's job*. I walk down the street quickly. I have work to do. I have a whole life to create and only twelve hours to do it in. I have to hurry if I'm going to be at the bar by nine.

KEY DROP

BY TOM LIPINSKI
Lawrenceville

The uphill turn at Butler and 44th Street is a tight one. The sudden and steep incline is further complicated by an already thin roadway that is parked solid at both curbs, holding the overflow from the shops on Butler—shops that change hands from convenience stores, pizza shops, barbers, and on to simple and inviting coffee spots with each pass.

Dorsey maneuvered the old Buick through the intersection, taking care with the long front grille and bumper, hoping not to sideswipe a car parked at the corner, then squeezed the accelerator, prepping the engine for the climb. He kept an eye out for a parking spot but found none, only open spaces reserved with kitchen table chairs planted at the curb, so pulled to his right into a church lot. The church was a dark and imposing brick and Dorsey recalled his last few visits to 44th, reminding himself that it was a Polish congregation. Now what the hell was the name of that burned-up painting of the Madonna they had hanging in there?

He climbed out of the car, stretched himself to his full six feet plus, and caught a touch of summer breeze. After waiting for traffic to pass, he hustled across the street to a line of row houses with minute front yards enclosed in black wrought-iron fencing. As Dorsey undid the gate latch the front door swung open and emitted an airborne wave of gray and sudsy wash water.

"The hell is that?" Dorsey retreated to the edge of the sidewalk. "Hell of a greeting. Ask me to stop by, make it sound important, and then this."

"Just finished the hall floor," Mrs. Leneski told him, walking down her front stoop, metal slop bucket in her hand. She's old, Dorsey reminded himself, man is she old. Gracing the far end of her eighties, Mrs. Leneski flirted with five feet of height, apparently so frail that a light rain could wash her, and the last of her gray hair pulled tight to the skull, down the street. She had on a sleeveless housedress that came to the midcalf and did nothing to hide the dark electronic ring that encircled her right ankle.

"Should've never shot that guy," Dorsey said, looking toward her feet. "Lucky this is all they did to you, even at your age."

"I asked you to do it," Mrs. Leneski replied, turning over her bucket and draining the last of the water. Her voice held the last traces of a childhood spent in Eastern Europe. "Right in that kitchen, over coffee. You said no. And you had enough good reasons to do it too. So, that left me."

Determined not to go over old and painful ground once again, Dorsey asked how she was getting along. "*Tak sobie*, so-so. Thing on my ankle gives me a rash. Thank God they still make the Noxzema cream."

Dorsey gave her a soft grin. "So, are you asking me in? Maybe some coffee?" He stepped through the gate and took the bucket from her hand. "Want to tell me what this is about? Why you asked me over?"

"Sure, sure, down to business," Mrs. Leneski said, turning to go into the house. "Mr. Detective wants to know about the case. Still call it that?'

"Sometimes," Dorsey said, trailing behind her. "What's on your mind?"

Mrs. Leneski stopped at the threshold and turned. "First, you take me shopping. I need a few things."

"They let you go out?" Dorsey asked. "Somebody you have to call first? Maybe the probation office?"

Dorsey was watching her shake her head when he noticed something on the street had caught her eye. He turned and scanned the street, the only thing moving was an immaculate black Cadillac heading up the street.

"You see that? The undertaker?" Mrs. Leneski asked, looking up at Dorsey. "He steals."

"What do you mean, he steals?"

"You know, he's an undertaker," she told him. "Shoes, socks, sometimes even suits. You think anybody really goes into the ground with a new pair of shoes on their feet?"

Standing behind the shopping cart in the produce section, Dorsey watched the old woman examine cabbage head after cabbage head, and recounted to himself the story behind this cockeyed friendship. She hires you, a few years back when no one was sending you work, to find her missing granddaughter. "She's with them junkies in the park," she had told him. She had been close, the girl was on the far side of a wrecked fence that separated the park from a cemetery. Four feet down and no marker except for a plain of broken beer and wine bottles to cover some tracks. You found her all right, and you found out who killed her. "But I can't prove it," you had told her, "not enough for the DA or the cops." "So," Mrs. Leneski had said, "then you kill him for me. I'll give you a bonus." But you just shook your head and left the house, and left the woman to do the killing herself. And with some back door legal tricks, an eighty-some-year-old gets house arrest and a metal band on her ankle for a killing.

214 // Pittsburgh Noir

Four heads proved good enough to make it into the cart and Dorsey asked how many people she was cooking for. "Somebody will show up," she told him. "They always do when I make halupki."

"Polish hand grenades?"

"Irish wise-ass," Mrs. Leneski said, and pulled on the front of the cart, directing him to the checkout lanes. "Ziggy gets the meat for me down The Strip. And a few other things. He'll be by later."

Dorsey began angling the cart toward a checkout line but Mrs. Leneski took hold of the front and dragged him into another aisle. "Not her," she said, indicating a young girl behind a register. "She cheats people, charges double on things like meat sometimes. She has something going with the manager, they're in it together."

"Not hot enough, not yet, for iced tea," Mrs. Leneski said, putting a cup of coffee on the Formica tabletop in front of Dorsey. They were in her kitchen now and despite a thorough going over, Dorsey could find nothing that had changed since his last visit. Refrigerator and oven still the same off-white, the sink a stand-alone with plumbing exposed. Except for a few newly acquired blemishes, even the coffee cups looked the same. Dorsey hoped her problems had changed.

He took a sip of unusually strong coffee. "So," he said, lowering the cup to the table. "Time to tell me why I'm here. Must have someone else to take you shopping."

Mrs. Leneski took a seat across the table from him. "You remember last time, last time you met my Catherine?"

Dorsey remembered. "Met her just the once. And she wasn't doing so well. I met her up the street at the old hospital. She was in the east wing, the psych ward?"

She had been in her midforties then, and detoxing for the third time. Dorsey recalled the incoherent voice that could barely recall she had a daughter of her own. *The one you found dead.* "She clean these days?" Dorsey asked.

"So they say," Mrs. Leneski said. "In a way, I guess. She's on her own, has a little place about ten blocks over on Carnegie Street, the other ward. And she's got this job, but it's a job with bad people, I think."

Dorsey sipped at his coffee. "What kind of work? For who?"

"One of them new places, the new ones along Butler Street, you've seen them. All those coffee shops, they make little sandwiches and crap for lunch, try to sell the art right off the walls? She's at one of them near 37th Street across from where the Catholic high school was."

"That I remember," Dorsey said, recalling a visit there while searching for the granddaughter. Girls in uniform trying to slip things past nuns in habits. "Thought those sorts of places were popular around here now."

"Some are, I guess," Mrs. Leneski said, dismissing the idea with a wave of her hand. "She works for one of the Predic family, he owns the place where she makes the sandwiches, waits on the table. The Predics, the whole family is no good."

"Do they steal like the undertaker or cheat like the checkout girl at the supermarket?" Dorsey asked from behind his raised coffee cup. "Sorry, it had to be asked."

Mrs. Leneski left her chair and went to the sink, turning her back to him. "She's old and she's crazy, that's what you think. Like I think people are all out to get me." She turned to face him. "I just know things, things and people. They're up to something at that place Catherine works. Damned Predics. I'd go there myself and find out but I have this thing on my ankle. So you have to go."

* * *

So you have to go, Dorsey reminded himself, cruising across Carnegie Street, checking for the address on the slip of paper Mrs. Leneski had given him. Thirty years you've been out of the army, and you're still intimidated by anything that sounds like a direct order. "And another thing, she only lives thirteen blocks from work, and she takes the bus along Butler. Thirteen blocks and she pays bus fare, can't walk to work. Wastes her money. You find out what's going on at that place and get her out of there."

Dorsey moved along Carnegie in the Buick, the brown brick of the homes and front porches giving away to the red brick of St. Kieran's Church. Just past the rectory, he pulled to the curb and killed the engine, focusing his attention on the house bearing the address he was looking for, apparently transformed from a one-family residence into two apartments. Dorsey checked out the second-story windows where Catherine was said to live. Windows closed and curtains drawn despite the afternoon warmth, the place was unremarkable and Dorsey considered putting in some surveillance time but decided against it. It'll get you nowhere, he thought, best that could happen is you fall into a nap and end up with a sore lower back. Better to get some questions answered first. He twisted the ignition key, rolled over the engine, and proceeded a few more blocks and through one last intersection. At the corner was a low-slung building fronted by a large yard done over in cement and brick, the local AOH club, the only marker a small sign tacked above the front door. A buzzer and card slot was mounted next to the doorjamb and Dorsey depressed the button. The door was opened by a short man wearing a bartender's double-wrapped apron.

"Lookin' for Danny?"

Dorsey said that he was and the man waved him into a small vestibule followed by a wide barroom with tables and matching chairs scattered across the floor. "Danny," the bartender called to a far corner. "Guy here for you."

At the corner table was a thin, older man dressed in gray work pants and a sport shirt, paging his way through the newspaper. On the tabletop was a can of ginger ale, a glass with cracked ice, and a freshly opened pack of Chesterfields. When the man raised his head of white hair, Dorsey saw the blue eyes and lean good features of the Sullivan clan, his mother's people. The slow grin reminded Dorsey that this was one of the few who had managed to hold onto his original teeth.

"How's things, Uncle Danny?"

"Calling me uncle, huh?" the man joked. "You must be in some kind of trouble. Better sit down and tell me."

"Trouble? I imagine so," Dorsey said, taking the seat across the table. "Just not sure what kind it might be." Dorsey motioned at the Chesterfields. "Thought you gave them up."

"I don't smoke 'em," Uncle Danny answered, pulling one from the pack. "Don't even light them up. Just gives me something to do with my hands. I still have to pay for 'em, but I save money on the matches." He toyed with the smoke for a moment. "Always good to see you, don't get me wrong, but something must've brought you over here."

"Had to take an old lady cabbage shopping." Dorsey waived down the bartender, ordered two more ginger ales, and brought his uncle up to date on his afternoon.

Uncle Danny toyed with a Chesterfield. "Between 36th and 37th? Right on Butler?" He laughed for a moment. "Might be the old whorehouse."

"There was a whorehouse there?"

"Not much of one," he told Dorsey, "not that I was ever in

there, let's get that straight. But you're saying this shop is just across Butler from the old high school?"

Dorsey said that it was.

Uncle Danny laughed. "That's who told me about it, the kids at the school. Some of my neighbors' kids went to school there, and kids, they pick up on everything. From what they tell me, they'd be in algebra or typing class, look out the window across the street, and they'd see some guy ringing the bell at a door. Not the storefront door, but the one next to it that leads to the apartments on the second floor, know what I mean?"

Dorsey sipped at the ginger ale and nodded for his uncle to go on.

"Anyways," Uncle Danny said, "nobody answers the door but a window on the second floor opens up and a woman kind of a pokes her head out. From what I hear she was stripped to her bra, in good weather. If she recognizes the guy she sends down the door key on a cord, the guy unlocks the door and goes inside. Then the woman in the window yanks up the cord and key and they're off to the races."

"Can't imagine Catherine being able to make a living that way," Dorsey told him. "Haven't seen her in more than few years, but still."

"In that business, the level of the clientele determines the level of the talent." Uncle Danny set down the unlit smoke. "There're sad old men and horny boys that ain't so choosey."

"I just don't see it," Dorsey said, shaking his head. "Tell me about these people, the Predics."

It was Uncle Danny's turn to shake his head. "Some families, I just don't know, the kids are wild. Can't say it was the parents, the old man had a nice business doing cement work, and the mother was okay. Kids were another story. Maybe it's the house they live in, as if the walls tell them to be nuts. All the boys, and there was a slew of them, they start out at the Catholic school, and by sixth grade they are tossed out to the public school. And high school, don't even give it a thought. So, some dope and drink and then vandalism. And then burglary when they finally figure out that if you don't just destroy property, but instead haul it away and sell it to someone, you can actually make some money."

"Anything recent?"

"I'm sure there is, but I haven't heard of it," Uncle Danny said. "And if one of them has a lunchroom, he's selling more than whole wheat sandwiches and sprout salads."

Dorsey thanked his uncle and got to his feet, heading for the door.

"Better wait a second," Uncle Danny called out, stopping him. "If this Predic boy is the one I'm thinking of, the two of you have an acquaintance in common."

Dorsey turned. "How's that?"

"The big ape you had trouble with a few years back, the one everyone calls Outlaw? He's close with the sons. Remember him, right?"

"I remember."

"You should—last time you shot him in the foot," Uncle Danny said. "If you get the chance, do us all a favor and shoot him in the other foot."

By quarter past nine, the key had made four trips from the second-floor window, attached to green electric wire and let out by Catherine Leneski. Dorsey was sure of it, despite the gray in her hair and the sag of her chin. While he watched there had been two couples with children in strollers, one young fellow carrying a toddler, and a young girl chasing a three-year-old. Each had knocked at the door, the window had been raised, and the key dangled. Each had gone inside for a short bit and then left, none with children.

Dorsey was across Butler, relaxing behind the steering wheel of the Buick. Traffic had been sporadic for the most part, punctuated by the passing of trailer trucks that used every inch of the street, causing Dorsey to wince each time one moved along. Part of the morning had been spent in front of a computer screen, confirming that Anthony Predic had purchased the building two years earlier at a rock-bottom price. The previous owner had been a shoemaker with his shop on the first floor. Dorsey wondered if the shoemaker had known what was going on upstairs all those years. He also wondered if the trick with the key had been on the deed. Now, across the street, when the trucks gave him a break, he watched a young man wash the storefront window of what was now The Boilermaker Lunchbox. From his vantage point, Dorsey could see a long serving counter with restored swivel stools, several large and well-shined coffee urns, and a line of booths at the far wall.

Behind the wheel he scratched a few comments into a notebook, the sort of thing he always did because he realized that in this business, the final report is everything. Send the report and attach the invoice, and hope that the report convinces the customer to pay the invoice. His notes described the people who had left their children. All had been working class, the two couples appearing to be stuck at the bottom of the scale. The men had the half beards of hoped-for maturity and wore old jeans, T-shirts with a hockey-playing penguin on them, and matching ball caps. The women wore the same outfits, but they somehow made them appear a bit more feminine. The single woman had been dressed in the white uniform that identified her as anything from a nurse to a waitress. It convinced Dorsey that the nursing profession should find itself new, and more specific, attire.

He dropped the notebook on the seat next to him and worked his back deeper into the upholstery. Why bother with notes? He reminded himself that after his last job with Mrs. Leneski, she had refused a written final report, but she had paid. As always, she was an exception. *And you, you figured she might be heading toward dementia.* The undertaker steals, the checkout girl cheats customers to get in good with the manager she's already sleeping with, and maybe the cabbage heads are talking to her. But Catherine has been nowhere near the serving counter all morning and instead is up to something on the second floor. Mostly shaky people knock on the door, she drops the key, in they go and come back without their kids. Nothing illegal in that—pretty goddamned weird, but not illegal.

Dorsey stayed on watch for another hour or so until one of the young couples who had been there earlier returned. The routine with the key was repeated, and they came back out with a child and stroller. Dorsey slipped out of the car, adjusted his sport shirt to cover the Glock he carried in a waistband holster, and crossed the street. He slipped by the young couple without a word and went into the Lunchbox.

"Where's the back steps?" Dorsey asked the young man behind the counter. "Tony and Outlaw said I ought to use the back way, not mess around with the key."

"Neither of them are here," the young man said, dunking coffee cups into a sink of blue water. "Want to wait? Supposed to be back in just a bit."

"I know all about that," Dorsey said, "but I'm supposed to wait up top."

222 // PITTSBURGH NOIR

Dorsey watched the young man's eyes dart about. C'mon, kid, buy into it.

"Maybe I should call them on the cell," the guy said.

"Fine by me, but I'm supposed to be looking over the second floor before they get back, understand?"

The man sighed. "C'mon, back this way. But I'm still gonna call."

He led Dorsey behind the counter and past the glass doors of a cooler stocked with sliced luncheon meats and into the backroom. There was a flight of steps to the left and as they climbed Dorsey asked the young man if he had to get ready for the lunch crowd.

"What there is of it," he answered, unlocking the door at the top of the steps. He pushed it open and stood aside. "But I still have to get it ready."

Dorsey wedged past him and heard the door being closed and locked behind him. He was in what had once been an apartment kitchen, no appliances but a large sink decorated with rust stains was attached to the far wall. Around it, three stacks deep, were sealed cardboard cartons. Dorsey looked them over and found flat screens, microwaves ovens, and a few Bose radios. He smiled. Don't look too bad for having fallen off the truck.

Out in a long hallway that ran the length of the building, Dorsey moved along listening to the sound of recorded music and children's singing voices. He passed a closed door and made his way to an open doorway at the front of the building, across the hall from the front staircase. Inside were two boys and a girl, topping out at age five, Dorsey figured, half asleep on the floor in front of a flat-screen TV. An animated story was playing out; a couple of bears were singing advice to a wide-eyed girl.

None of the kids took notice as Dorsey crossed the room to three cribs against the far wall, opposite the windows. One was empty but the other two held sleeping infants, apparently undisturbed by the singing. On the floor between two of the cribs was a kitchen food scale lying on its side, plastic baggies scattered around it. He heard some light footfalls in the hallway, turned, and saw Catherine walk into the room.

"Who the hell are you?" she said in a voice that was a bit angered but also bewildered. She wore jeans and a black T-shirt and her hair was matted back against the sides of her head. It was the eyes that Dorsey concentrated on. Half shuttered and high as a kite. "I didn't hear anyone knock."

"And you didn't send down the key," Dorsey responded. "Forgot about that part."

"That's right," she said. "The key."

Dorsey shook his head and turned to the children in front of the TV. He took two of them gently by the shoulder and tried to rouse them. All he got in return were two weak yawns. He turned back to Catherine.

"Doesn't really matter what you're on these days," Dorsey told her, settling his eyes on her face. "But what did you give these kids? And what are you doing with them?"

Catherine appeared to drift for a second. "Benadryl," she said. "Just a little. Keeps them quiet."

Dorsey stepped back to the cribs. "The infants too?"

"Oh yeah," she said. "They sleep for hours that way."

Jesus, Dorsey thought, day care for drugged-out parents. "What is it?" he asked her. "A young couple needs to get their heads straight, so they drop the kid off while they score?"

"Some."

And more than that, Dorsey realized, remembering the young woman in white. Poor, single, and working for a paycheck. But not one big enough to get legitimate child care. No family, no friends. The underground economy of stolen goods and drugs. Just add a little day care for the clientele. For a fee. And don't even think about what that might entail.

Dorsey took another look at one of the infants and started digging in his pocket for his cell. "Got a problem here," he told Catherine. "This kid's turning blue."

He started to punch in 911 when the young man from the Lunchbox came in from the hall. "In here," he called out. "Right in here." He pointed at Dorsey. "Better stay off that phone."

"Why?" Dorsey said. "You obviously didn't."

Despite the intervening years, Dorsey recognized the man as soon as he entered. He had a few inches of height on Dorsey, but it was the shoulders that told the tale. Twice Dorsey's width, Outlaw walked with a minor shuffle and Dorsey figured he hadn't forgotten how that came to be. Even worse, there was a Louisville Slugger, brightly shellacked and the grain jumping out, in his hands.

"Hank Aaron model?" Dorsey asked, hoping to throw off the big man. "Better get this straight, we got a sick kid on our hands, not-breathing-so-well sick. I'm calling for paramedics. Whatever you want to do with me can keep for later."

Outlaw grinned, pushed back his long black hair with his left hand, then dragged himself across the room and took his first swing. Dorsey ducked and fell back to the wall, surprised that he was more concerned with protecting the cell than his own body. The swing was wild and Outlaw lost his balance for a moment, but just that. While he righted himself, Dorsey got to the Glock at his hip.

"Hold on," he told Outlaw, pointing the gun to the floor. "I'll shoot you. Just to be a prick, I'll shoot you in your other foot. Okay?"

Outlaw hesitated for a moment, then went at him. Dorsey straightened his elbow and fired. He looked down at Outlaw, checked out Catherine and the Lunchbox guy. "Now," Dorsey told them all, punching numbers into the cell, "I'm making a phone call. All right with everybody?"

"Not the same foot?" Uncle Danny asked. "You shot him in the other foot?"

They were back at the table, a ginger ale each.

"The other foot," Dorsey told him. "Just like you asked."

OVERHEARD

BY REGINALD MCKNIGHT
Homewood

That's the thing about this town, Merce: you cross one street—the right side of the street—and you've crossed over to a whole other world. Do I have to tell you this? You know. You own property everywhere your dad was allowed to buy. So-called Homewood One and so-called Homewood Two are separate planets, no closer than Earth and Pluto.

I told you what that dude Matt said to me the first week Colleen and the boy and I moved into our place on Lang—

Yes I did, man—

I did, Merce. You never—

All right, so he walks up to me while I'm out front sweeping the walk, and he says, "Welcome to the neighborhood," and he says his name is Matt, and he lives right over there across the street. Points with his rake.

I had a broom. Him, he'd been raking. Sweeping, raking, very neighborhoody behavior, right?

Yes! He was white. Of course he was white. That's my—

Merce, just listen to me, okay? Follow along, man, and I'll

tell you all this stuff about the girl getting beaten, and what I think happened upstairs, and what this has to do with my rent.

Man, I have never in my life missed rent. I been late once or twice, but . . .

So this guy Matt points with his rake and squints at me like he's got battery acid in his eyes, and smiles like it hurts, and he shrugs at me and goes . . . How does he put it? "So we were just wondering why you all chose Point Breeze instead of the actual Homewood for a place to settle." Something like that, see? And by "we," he means the people up and down Lang, dig?

It took me a couple beats to gather this. At first I thought he was talking about just him and his own brood, but when he starts talking about what the DelGrossos had to say, and the Millers, and so forth, I see he's talking about person-to-person, house-to-house, what the whole village—idiots included, apparently—thought about us moving in next to them. Instead of the proper one.

Dude, listen to me. I'm not from here. I grew up on military bases. We been a-integratin' since before I was born: '47, '48. What the fuck do I know about living on the right side of the street?

Actually, no. He said about eighty percent of them were cool with us living there. I mean, yeah, it creeped me out that they actually clustered their heads together and practically voted on it, but yeah, they did vote us in, I guess you could say.

Where? Dancing Goats.

* * *

Dancing Goats? The place on Ellsworth, near—

Yeah, that's the one. I don't know. Coffee's coffee, right?

No, it wasn't that. Lang Avenue didn't help the marriage, but that wasn't the reason. I told you the reason.

Yeah.

And for your information, I didn't move into the real Home-wood because I've learned to agree with guys like Matt. I took your place because it's huge and beautiful: lots of wood, full of light, high ceilings. It's nice and quiet, except for, you know . . . But I'll get to that in a minute.

Three bedrooms. Three, for seven-fifty, and manageable utilities. I'm like six blocks from the Lang place but I feel far enough away from Colleen and Brian not to hurt all the time.

I know, I know, you don't keep tabs on old girlfriends with-out paying the price. I know what I did. Half the puddles I wept into your nice carpet and wood were from shame and embarrassment. The other half were because I missed Brian so much.

Yeah, yeah, I know you guys did too. You know it's compli-cated, yeah. That's why I guess I hardly noticed the people upstairs, at first. It's the usual thing with couples who live above you. You hear their bedsprings, you hear him raise his voice or punch a wall; sometimes the music is a bit too loud, but she keeps it down. You hear them shower and flush, and hang pictures, stack dishes. Pretty soon you know the difference between his footfall and hers. Everybody's pretty much the same.

No-no-no, that's not my point. The thing is, they weren't all that noisy. I used to live below a couple of opera singers in Colorado Springs. That was much worse.

I'm serious. No, they made normal noises, for the most part, and when Brian isn't with me, it kind of made me feel a little less alone. Besides, I have this big-ass air filter in my bedroom . . . Of course, you've seen it. Duh. Anyway, I usually run it all night, and it whites out the universe.

No, I hardly ever thought about Tamara and that guy, but like this one night? Brian was with me? And we'd had a very cool weekend. We'd watched *The Lion King* for like the eight millionth time. He spent all day in that ridiculous lion costume, roaring at people in the mall, at The Strip, Frick Park. But anyway, the weekend's almost done, so of course I'm depressed. The filter's on, cause I don't want to hear them having sex; I don't want to hear sirens, nothing. Brian's in his room long asleep, and I'm tipped that way myself. It's, like, two.

Brian taps on my door. "Papa." Barely hear him, but I'm up. "There's a loud noise," he says. He points to the ceiling. I shut off the filter and we listen. I hear thumping out in the stairway. I walk Brian back to his room, go out into the hallway, and see them both at the bottom of the stairs at the entrance. Tamara's sitting on the last step, with her arms over her head, and boyfriend's standing over her, trying to whale on her, but he's being patient, like a boxer. He wants her face, not her arms. First time I'd seen him, actually. He's got the tan

Timberland boots, the baggy pants, hoodie, watch cap. He's beating a woman. Very disappointing.

He's in midswing, and she's swollen under the eye and bleeding from the nose. I say, "Tamara, you all right?" And asshole turns around and says, "What you need, bitch?" But I look past him and repeat myself. Tamara says, "Can you call the cops?"

"Already have," I said, which wasn't true, but I figured it'd cool the asshole, which it did. He slams out the door, and by that time, at the bottom of the stairs, Tamara's on her feet. I lock the front door and walk her back up to her own door. I ask her if she needs anything. She tells me no, but I just stand there for a while, not sure if I should walk her down to my place for first aid, or ice, or whatever.

You ever notice how beautiful she is? Cause I really hadn't till then. I mean, I'd seen her a dozen times or so, more or less up close, at the mailbox, mostly, or passing on the stairway. But I'd never stood so close and face-to-face. She smells like gardenias and some kind of sweet spice. I like those almond eyes, the long lashes, her skin. It's like smooth and the color of pecans. I mean, you have to be blind not to notice the hourglass body, but even with the swollen eye, the face is like love, like art.

Yeah, well, if it's conventional it ain't beauty.

Yeah, actually did call, when I went back down to my place. They showed up fairly quickly and I'm not sure my boy would have gone back to sleep at all if I hadn't lain there with him for a while as the two of us watched the blue lights flash across the walls and ceiling.

* * *

Couldn't tell you. We both slept till about nine.

All right, so I got back from dropping off the son, and there's Tamara and this portly dark-skinned woman outside the landing in front of her door—her second door. You know, the one that—

Yeah. They were trying to fix it, see?

No, they weren't changing the goddamn lock, Merce. The thing just doesn't work, okay?

Can you blame these folks? How does she know you're not one of those landlords who shine you on, put you off, blow you back, toss you out? You get used to things running a certain way in your world and you don't bother.

Exactly. Let me go on. This isn't about you.

I know I owe you money, but let me tell you what happened, all right? There are some things bigger than your money.

I know, I know, but listen.

They were actually having a good time. Giddy, giggling with frustration, seemed to me. "What are y'all up to?" I asked them, and Tamara smiles at me like I'm some kind of super Jesus and says, "Can you fix this, Reggie?" and I winced a little, but let it go, that *Reggie*, and just said back, "Did he break in?"

"Last night?" she said. "Naw, I let him in."

Her friend says, "You don't even need no credit card to open this door."

And Tamara said, "You could blow on it and it'll just lay open like a ho."

"Girl," her friend said, "you going to hell for that one!"

I told them I'd be back up in a second with my toolbox, and I was back up in two seconds. The only problem was the thing was loose, every—

All the plates and stuff, and needed a little machine oil. It was tight, and the only thing that could open it was the key. I told Tamara to buy a slap bolt for the inside, and I'd put it on for her, if they needed me to.

Don't mention it, man. Oh yeah, I forgot to tell you I'd been wearing sandals that day. And while the women were watching me work, Tamara said, "Dee, don't he have some pretty feet, for a man?"

"You got that right, Tam. They some pretty dogs. For a man? Sheeit, I'd trade him straight up."

"Reggie, how you get them feet?"

I know, what was I supposed to say, Footlocker, morgue, Mom and Dad, Homewood Cemetery?

Right, right, right: *Well, you know how you just see feet slung up over telephone lines and on roadsides? Yeah, they're all over the damn place. Take 'em home; throw 'em in the washer, presto! Lady's feet, mahogany, good as new!*

Anyway, it was quiet for two weeks, and I didn't hear her come or go. Little music, TV off or turned down low after eleven, as per your lease agreement. Come to think of it, she was living pretty much as she had before the guy started coming around.

Hadn't even thought about how quiet she'd been at first. I got to figuring she was from a good home. I mean, she dressed well for her job, rarely worked the cleavage in her play clothes. But it was more than that. There was something . . . I don't know, *pristine* about her. Yeah, that's the word. I didn't think she "belonged" here any more than me. Very middle class, I suppose.

She does? Okay, that proves my point. Everyone from there may know his name, or how famous he is, and they know he wrote a ton of books about Homewood, but few actually read him. Interesting.

I stopped using my fan. I was, you know, on alert, worried about her. Wanted to hear every sound. That's why I heard all this horrible stuff last weekend.

No, he wasn't there, thank God.

No, every *other* weekend.

Tell me about it.

The whole thing was so eerie because there were no voices. No arguing or screaming. There wasn't any music, no Tupac, no Snoop, no Biggie, just hard tympanic thumps. The walls. Soles and heels rolled like thunder across my ceiling. In fact, that's what woke me. Thought it was a storm. I lay there in the dark, Merce, and I hear knees and elbows splintering. You could hear the cracks and ghost strokes radiating back into the intermittent silence. You could hear furniture scraping across the floor. Something made of glass shattered, and pieces of it rattled and tumbled and skittered across the wood.

Walls boomed; the whole frame shook and it was a good while before I picked up the phone.

Well, I don't know, exactly, but I'm lying there and the phone's, like, a fucking foot from my head, and I'm actually taking the time to think, *He's killing her up there.*

I picked up the phone and the noise quit like someone'd thrown a mattress over it. Only thing I could hear was my ears and temples knocking. My blood rocked my whole body. I didn't press a single button, not a nine or a one, and the thing began to bleat to be hung up, and it sounded like it was loud enough for him to hear it upstairs, so I hung it up, sat up, and listened. So, as my heart slowed, I could hear normally, more or less. Car engines, tires, woofers, tweeters. I heard drunken boys making like magpies as they walked past my window. One of them's going, "Yeah, yeah, yeah, and it's like he don't even know when to stop and listen, so like I'm all up in his grille . . ." and as the boy's voice fades, I hear in its place this low, steady, "Uh-uh-uh-uh," and I mean it's constant, but I can't tell whether it's a man or a woman. I can't tell anything about it, but it goes on for a long, long, long, long time, and I'm pinned down there on my bed and pretty soon I tell myself they're having sex, and I should mind my own business, and I got a right to be disgusted and pissed off and a right to some peace and quiet and sleep. I turn on the filter. I slept.

I'd have slept till noon or better if not for the smell of ammonia that socked me awake at about seven. No mystery as to why they use that stuff for smelling salts. I got up, stepped into my pants, walked the hallway from bedroom to kitchen. I stepped to the back window and gazed through the bars and dirty glass and down the fire escape. The ammonia drew tears from my eyes and I wiped them with my wrist. A nasty film ate at my throat. My feet didn't quite touch the ground.

Down by the big blue dumpster, I saw this trim black boy of seventeen or so: trench coat, hoodie, Timberlands. The uniform, you dig?

He may or may not have been carrying, but who's gonna ask? The suit makes the A-bomb. But other than the getup, there was nothing actually sinister about him—no shades or grim visage. All he did was nod at the cars that rolled by the dumpster like he was the town sheriff, and when people came by with their garbage, he smiled, nodded, said a couple words, even bowed a little, pointed nowhere in particular with his thumb. Every single person walked back home carrying their trash. No back talk, no heat, and no questions. I wasn't a bit surprised, Merce, even though it was garbage day.

And I can't say I was surprised by the first of three men carrying the black leaf bags down the fire escape. I already know because I've seen the movies, read the books. Ammonia tells you one thing, trench coats tell you the other, the only thing next is black garbage bags. But I don't mean to sound blasé about it. I wasn't. Not a bit. For every step the first guy took down the steps, I took a step away from the window. I realized that the sound I'd heard at the tail end of my night hadn't been sex at all, and I guess I already knew that even then, before I flicked on the air filter. It was the sound of someone dying, of someone laboring with a handsaw over flesh and bone.

Uh-huh, backed up all the way till my ass met the little olive stove and amber-yellow fridge. Turned around and looked at them—clean, familiar acquaintances of mine. I grabbed the handle of the fridge, but didn't pull it open. I looked at the stovetop, the teapot, the coffee maker and toaster, and for a couple seconds I couldn't remember what they were called or what they were for. Turned back around in time to see the second bag make its unmistakably butcher-shop way down the fire escape. I got this galvanic *zap* on the back of my tongue. You know, like when you're a kid and stupid enough to lick the anodes of a nine-volt battery. It was a kind of supercharged horror I could taste. My body, like, just dumped sweat—all at once, from every pore. I'm hot; I'm shivering. I crept back to the window as the third bag made its way down. The boy held the lid open, the guy tossed the bag in, and the boy lowered the lid. All of them stood next to the dumpster and smoked till the truck came, but I can't remember whether they walked, drove, or flew away.

No, Merce. I did not call the cops.

Well now, see, that's what I called to tell you. I'm not a bit surprised she's paid her rent, because day before yesterday, she came to my place.

Yes, Tamara.

Of course I was stunned, man, are you kidding? I'd spent days feeling her ghost in my mouth. After showers, I sit on the edge of the tub and stare at my feet.

Yeah, my feet.

Talk about not eating. Talk about insomnia and silence and emptiness. I thought divorce was . . . I thought nothing could be worse than those days when I first moved into your place and ate cobwebs and pissed blood, and cried piss, and bayed like a hound every night Brian wasn't under my roof.

And then one day she's standing at my door as beautiful as a palm full of tea roses and asking me can she come in. I let her in. Says she's been away for a while, and only back in town to get a few things. Told me the boyfriend had tried to break in a few days back, and she'd had to leave to find a new place. Said he was crazy, dealt drugs, killed people, feared nothing. She shook, she cried; her voice quavered just perfectly. She asked me for money for a bus back out of town and a hotel, till her new place was ready. Said she'd pay me back in a week, maybe two.

Of course I didn't believe her.

Of course I gave her the money.

Three hundred bills, dude.

That's why I called you, man.

ABOUT THE CONTRIBUTORS

K.C. CONSTANTINE has had seventeen novels published by four different publishers. Publishers, retailers, and reviewers persist in their opinion that these are "mysteries" because the main characters are mostly cops and sometimes one or two characters get arrested. He's given up trying to tell them otherwise. He's also had two stories published in anthologies edited by Otto Penzler. His story included here is his third and probably his last because stories are hard and the pay is bad.

Cayce Ellison

CARLOS ANTONIO DELGADO earned his MFA from the University of Pittsburgh and won the 2008 Turow-Kinder Fiction Award for the first two chapters of his novella, *The Voice and Arms of God*. He has placed fiction in *The Ankeny Briefcase* and in *Relief Journal's* first annual *Best of Relief* anthology. He lives and works in Los Angeles—at Biola University's Torrey Honors Institute—but he misses his little brick house in the Morningside neighborhood of Pittsburgh.

Joseph Mertz

REBECCA DRAKE'S debut thriller, *Don't Be Afraid*, came out in September 2006 from Pinnacle. *The Next Killing* followed in September 2007 and was selected by four national book clubs including the Literary Guild. Her third novel, *The Dead Place*, came out in September 2008 and was an Independent Mystery Booksellers Association (IMBA) best seller. A former journalist and native New Yorker, Drake currently lives in Pittsburgh.

Hilary Masters

KATHLEEN GEORGE is a professor of theatre at the University of Pittsburgh. Her fourth novel, *The Odds*, was an Edgar Award finalist, and her previous work includes the novels *Taken, Fallen,* and *Afterimage*—all set in Pittsburgh and featuring Detective Richard Christie. She's also written books about theatre, the most recent of which is *Narrative and Drama*, and she has directed many plays.

Garrett Haines

KATHRYN MILLER HAINES is the author of two World War II–set mystery series: the Rosie Winter series for HarperCollins, and a young adult series for Roaring Brook Press, the first of which, *The Girl Is Murder*, is due out in 2011. A Texas native, she transplanted to Pittsburgh in 1994 and instantly developed a love for french fries and cole slaw on her sandwiches. She has lived in the Wilkinsburg neighborhood for the past fourteen years.

Yona Harvey

TERRANCE HAYES is the 2010 recipient of the National Book Award in poetry. His most recent collection is *Lighthead*. His other books are *Wind in a Box, Muscular Music,* and *Hip Logic.* His honors include four *Best American Poetry* selections, a Whiting Writers Award, a National Endowment for the Arts Fellowship, and a Guggenheim Fellowship. He is a professor of creative writing at Carnegie Mellon University and lives in Pittsburgh.

RDS: Madan

AUBREY HIRSCH'S stories, essays, and poems have appeared in several magazines including *Third Coast, Hobart, Vestal Review,* and the *Minnetonka Review.* Recent honors include a special mention as a finalist in Glimmer Train's Fiction Open and a nomination for a Pushcart Prize. She came to Pittsburgh for her MFA in creative writing and stayed for the bridges and cheese fries. She currently teaches creative writing in the MFA program at Chatham University.

Lauren Naefe

PAUL LEE was born in Hollywood, California. He attended UC Berkeley as an undergrad and earned his MFA from the University of Pittsburgh while living in Bloomfield and Friendship and sometimes a couch in the South Side. Currently he lives in Queens and is working on a novel.

Tom Altany

TOM LIPINSKI is a native of Pittsburgh and creator of the Carroll Dorsey mystery series. A Shamus Award winner, he has worked as a social worker, jail administrator, in auto repossessions, and as an insurance investigator. He holds an MFA from the University of Pittsburgh and a MA from Slippery Rock University, and is presently the chair of the English and theatre arts department at Edinboro University of Pennsylvania.

Archie Carpenter

NANCY MARTIN is the author of forty-eight novels in the mystery, suspense, historical, and romance genres. Nominated for the Agatha Award for Best First Mystery of 2002, *How to Murder a Millionaire* won the RT award for Best First Mystery. With the 2009 publication of *Our Lady of Immaculate Deception* from Minotaur, she launched a new Pittsburgh-based mystery series featuring Roxy Abruzzo. Martin currently lives in Pittsburgh and is a founding member of Pennwriters.

Hilary Masters

HILARY MASTERS moved into Pittsburgh's Mexican War Streets in 1984 when he joined the writing program at Carnegie Mellon University. His tenth novel, *Post*, will be published in 2011. In 2003 the American Academy of Arts and Letters granted his work its Award for Literature. Recently, the Independent Publishers Association awarded Masters its bronze medal for the literary short story.

Sabrina Orah Mark

REGINALD MCKNIGHT is the author of *The Kind of Light That Shines on Texas, White Boys, Moustapha's Eclipse, He Sleeps,* and *I Get on the Bus.* His many awards include the PEN/ Hemingway Special Citation, a Pushcart Prize, an O. Henry Award, the *Kenyon Review* Award for Literary Excellence, a Whiting Writers' Award, the Drue Heinz Literature Prize, and a fellowship from the National Endowment for the Arts.

Trudy O'Nan

STEWART O'NAN was born and raised and lives in Pittsburgh. His story collection, *In the Walled City*, received the Drue Heinz Literature Prize, and his first novel, *Snow Angels*, set in Butler, was recently made into a critically acclaimed film. Several of his dozen novels take place in Pittsburgh, including *Everyday People* (East Liberty) and the forthcoming *Emily, Alone* (Highland Park).

Robert Raysbich

LILA SHAARA is the author of *Every Secret Thing* and *The Fortune Teller's Daughter.* Trained as an anthropologist, she has held many jobs, including (in no particular order) disc jockey, radio talk show producer, secretary, bartender, waitress, "crew member" at a fast food chain, and high school teacher. Shaara teaches anthropology at a local university, and resides in Pittsburgh with her husband, two children, and many foundling pets.